Wheels—I love you, baby.

Acknowledgments

As I release the third book in the Playing For Keeps series, I want to take a moment to thank Crimson Romance for taking a chance on a five book series. There've been many hands who've touched this series, including Jennifer Lawler, Jess Verdi, Julie Sturgeon, Tara Gelsomino, and the cover artists who brought the sexy heroes to life with their talents. You all have made the experience of working with you a joy!

Playing for Hearts
BOOK THREE

Conveniently

Debra Kayn

Author of *Seductively* and *Wildly*

C R I M S O N
ROMANCE

F+W Media, Inc.

This edition published by
Crimson Romance
an imprint of F+W Media, Inc.
10151 Carver Road, Suite 200
Blue Ash, Ohio 45242
www.crimsonromance.com

ISBN 10: 1-4405-6651-8
ISBN 13: 978-1-4405-6651-6
eISBN 10: 1-4405-6652-6
eISBN 13: 978-1-4405-6652-3

Cover art © 123RF and istockphoto.com/technotr

Chapter One

Dana hitched up her dress, dodged the groups of people milling around in the lobby of Timber Lodge, and ran for the long hallway. A crowd had gathered in hopes of catching a glimpse of one of the U.S. men's downhill skiers, but what they'd gotten instead was a front row seat to the most humiliating moment of Dana's life. Positive the laughter in the room was at her expense, she only wanted to escape.

Escape from the embarrassment of wearing a wedding dress with no groom, no wedding, and no idea what she was going to do now.

A figure stepped in front of her exit. She bumped into a man's unmovable chest. Stumbling to the side, she gazed up into a pair of dark eyes. Her barricade stared at her intently, while holding her arms to keep her from falling.

"S-sorry," she mumbled, pulling away from him as he attempted to keep her there.

She spotted an open door, ran, and slipped into the empty banquet room. She gazed at the vases filled with pastel pink flowers atop the tables, the unlit candles, and the ivory colored lace draped over every flat surface. Everything perfectly decorated for a quaint reception. The guests who were coming had quietly slipped away after her fiancé, Jace Kendall, announced he'd changed his mind about getting married, because he wasn't in love with her anymore.

She removed the diamond necklace from the jewelry box that Jace had thrust into her hands, to soften the fact he'd dumped her on her wedding day, before he'd hightailed his way out the door. "I'm going to annihilate him."

She tossed the box to the floor, dug her phone out of the clutch purse she'd bought specifically for her wedding day—while dropping the jewelry inside—and rang her father. "Daddy. I've got an emergency and need you to do something for me."

"What's going on? You sound upset," her dad said. "Weren't you scheduled to get married right now?"

A knock sounded on the outer door. She raised her gaze, ignored the rude person interrupting her, and continued. "Jace walked out on me, said he didn't love me the way a man loves a woman and ... " she sniffed, "I want you to fire him. Kick him out of his office, and make sure someone else takes over his job."

"He's one of my best employees," her father said. "You'll get past this setback."

She squeezed her eyes closed and opened them again at the accusation in her dad's voice. "But, Daddy. *He* left *me.*"

The door opened and a man decked out in skiwear entered. He stood staring at her, and she glared while continuing to talk on the phone. "No, I don't want you to fly here from Italy." She paused to listen. "No, I don't want you to fly me away to Barbados. I want to get *married.* I want to become Mrs. Somebody today. That's what's supposed to happen. At twenty-five years old, I'm supposed to get married. At twenty-eight, I'm having my first baby. It's my life schedule, Daddy. You know how I've planned all the important events in my life. Jace ruined everything."

Her father sighed, sounding at a loss. "Do you want to come back home? I can send Pete there to run the shop."

Dana's father would never understand her need for order. Too busy traveling with his fourth wife and Dana's three half-brothers, he'd even failed to find time to attend the wedding of his only daughter from his first marriage. She blew out her breath. "No! No, I'm sorry I bothered you ... just go do whatever you're doing. I'll handle this myself. Bye, Daddy."

She disconnected the call and turned her attention to the man standing in the room with her. "What?"

"Are you okay?" He stepped forward, studying her in what appeared to be a mix of fascination and trepidation.

She grabbed her bodice and hitched her dress, squaring her shoulders. He acted as if he'd never seen a woman whose whole world had crumbled into a gazillion little pieces only moments ago. "I'm fine."

Dressed in a two-piece gray ski suit, with goggles sitting on the top of his head holding back shoulder-length black hair, he let his gaze take in the full length of her dress. His eyes, the color of mahogany, were heated and intense. A quiver traveled up her spine, not exactly unpleasant, but definitely unwanted. Right away, she pegged him for a player.

"If you're looking for the lobby, go out the door, turn right, and keep walking. You can't miss it. It's that huge room that's packed with everyone laughing and talking." She tapped her foot, itching to shed the dress and throw away anything that reminded her of Jace.

"I came here to check on you." He held his hands out to the sides of him. "I'm the guy you plowed into when you ran down the hallway. You looked like you were in trouble. I thought I'd see if I could help you with anything."

"There's nothing you can do for me except go." She kicked off her shoes and reached behind her, searching for the hidden zipper on the floor length, eggshell white gown she'd had specially made a year ago for this exact day. "You can leave and shut the door behind you."

He tilted his head. "You're shaking. Are you sure you're all right?"

"Yes, dammit." She grabbed her elbow and forced her other hand further down her back, trying to reach the tiny hook on her dress. "This is all Jace's fault."

"Who?"

She clamped her lips together and muffled her scream. Her eyes burned with unshed tears, and anger bubbled to the surface. She would not cry.

"What can I do?"

"Nothing," she snapped.

He tilted his head and his gaze dropped to her dress. "Babe ... let me help. You're upset."

She studied him for a few blinks, turned around, and presented him with her back. "Fine. Undo my zipper for me, but hurry. I feel like I'm going to be sick, and I hate throwing up."

Her need to remove any remembrance of her planned marriage trumped any modesty she may have felt over standing in her underwear in front of a man she'd never met before. She wiggled her shoulders in impatience. "Please, hurry."

"I'll have you out of here in no time." His hand skimmed her back as he deftly undid her dress, including the eyehooks.

She shivered, blaming the chill on her emotions, and shimmied out of the wedding dress. The material pooled at her feet, and she was finally free from the suffocating dress that reminded her of everything she'd lost today. She glanced down at her body. The five-hundred dollar lingerie set that'd arrived yesterday from her stepmother was all wrong. There was nothing sacred or pure about her thoughts at the moment.

A low whistle reminded her she wasn't alone and the man wasn't leaving. She sighed in self-pity, because trouble seemed to keep jumping out and tripping her lately. She couldn't get a break.

Not in the mood to deal with another skier whose only goal was to screw every snow bunny that flooded the lodge this time of year, Dana tried to ignore him in hopes he'd go away. During the workweek, she had lots of practice pushing away the attention of men. Running the shop downstairs put her right in line to deal with every male in the lodge.

Except, as she paced the banquet room, she couldn't help glancing at the man who'd stayed to help her.

He was one of the sexiest skiers she'd seen visit the lodge. The long black hair hung haphazardly to his shoulders, the patch of whiskers under his lower lip accented full lips, and dark eyes surrounded with even darker lashes made him drool-worthy. Normally, his looks would've grabbed her attention.

If she didn't hate every single man on Earth at this moment.

She planted her hands on her bare hips. "You've had your fill. There's no more to see, so you can leave."

He seemed to gaze at her ivory colored lingerie with too much interest. She half turned. If he said one thing about the garter belt, the pantyhose, or her lack of clothing, she'd stab him with her four-inch Jimmy Choos.

He took a step toward her and stopped. "You're crying."

"I am not." She swiped her cheeks, upset to find wetness. She never cried. Not since she was twelve and broke her arm at Mount Shasta during ski camp.

He reached into the back pocket of his ski pants and extracted a handkerchief. She sniffed. Crying over Jace was a waste of good tears. She should be putting this energy into a backup plan.

"May I?" the skier whispered, motioning with the cloth, then stepping forward when she refused to answer and dotting her cheeks dry.

She gazed into his eyes and was surprised to find only concern. "What kind of man carries a handkerchief?"

"One that never knows if he'll meet a beautiful woman who'll need one." His gaze softened.

"Really?"

"No." His mouth curved upward. His perfect white teeth practically sparkled. "I use one to clean the moisture out of my goggles when I ski."

She wrinkled her nose. "Please tell me this doesn't have your sweat on it."

"Don't worry. I haven't hit the slopes yet."

"Oh." She dropped her gaze. "Well, thank you. That wasn't necessary, but it was ... nice."

He hooked his thumb under her chin and lifted her gaze. "Will you be okay?"

The tenderness in his voice and the gentle touch undid her. She threw herself at him, burying her face in his neck, and sobbed.

She cried for her disappointing day, her pathetic wedding with no family and only the acquaintances from her father's business present to wish her well. Most of all she mourned for her failed life.

"Shh." He rubbed her back. "It can't be all bad."

Aware of the heat from the palm of his hand, Dana cried harder for her lost opportunity. She'd planned her life down to the most minuscule details in an effort to make sure she never ended up the way her parents had. Now it was over, and she had no idea what she was supposed to do next.

"Do you want to tell me what happened?" The man leaned back and held her by the upper arms, not letting her go.

"It doesn't matter. There's nothing I can do about it, not that I want to have that jerk back in my life." She blew her nose with the borrowed handkerchief. "Thanks for the shoulder and the h-handkerchief."

"My name's Juan."

"Dana." She inhaled a deep breath to compose herself. "I appreciate the help with the dress ... and the hug. I'm okay now."

Juan frowned. She moistened her lips and tilted her head. He seemed familiar. Probably one of the men she'd sold equipment to, or passed by on her way downstairs in the lodge on her way to work over the last couple of months.

"Listen, I don't want to leave you while you're upset." He glanced around the room. "Why don't you put the dress back on, and I'll buy you a drink at the bar. It'll help you relax."

"Ugh." She walked over and sat atop a table pushed up against the wall. "I don't want to wear that *thing* ever again. I don't care if I have to walk up to my room wearing … " she raised her arms, "nothing. I refuse to have anything to do with Jace Kendall. Do you know him? Because I wouldn't be against you taking a bat to his car or decking him."

"No, I don't recognize the name." Juan cleared his throat. "You should forget about him. It sounds like you're better off with him out of your life."

"Yes, I am." But she didn't believe it. Jace had been the answer to her prayers for the last two years. "I suppose I better go up to my room."

"Dressed like that?" His brows rose.

"I'm not touching the wedding dress." She pointed to the floor where the yards and yards of expensive lace lay discarded. "Besides, I'm hideous."

"You're lovely, and I don't think walking out there into the lodge is wise considering the place is filled to capacity with men desperate to look at a beautiful woman."

"I doubt that." She shrugged. "Don't you think if men were willing to be with me, I would've gotten married today instead of being dumped at the front door?"

Juan winced. "He's a fool."

"He didn't even wait until we stepped in front of the minister before he chickened out. He screwed up my whole life. If I don't get married today, I'll never be able to reach my next goal."

He made a sympathetic noise.

"Not only that, Now I'm probably never going to experience what it's like to have a hon—" She clamped her lips together, then mumbled, "Never mind."

Juan shrugged off his coat, walked over, and sat beside her. She shook her head, unwilling to believe she was sitting here, when she should be slipping upstairs to enjoy her honeymoon. Jace could rot in hell for all she cared.

"Here. Cover up. You're shaking." Juan slipped his coat over her shoulders. "I've already missed most of my slope time. You can borrow my coat."

She pushed the sleeves of the coat to her wrists, noticing it was one of her daddy's products. "Thanks. I'm sure I won't be the only woman caught running up the back stairs in her panties. I run into at least one woman a week sneaking out of the rooms the Olympic team uses."

"Is that so?" He unzipped his pants. "You can wear these too, I have spandex underneath. It'll be safer. No one looks at a man half undressed going up the back stairs."

"I don't know why you're being so nice to me." Dana sighed. "But I do appreciate it. I'm not the spoiled brat Jace said I was. He was just ... "

"An asshole?" He cussed, struggling with his zipper.

"Yes. Incredibly stupid and egotistical too." She glanced down at the front of his pants. "What's wrong?"

"Damn thing's stuck."

She pushed his hands aside. "It's the zipper. Happens all the time. Metal zippers rust over time, especially when subjected to the moist, cold weather the clothing is intended for ... big mistake. That's why Reese Enterprise uses plastic or coated zippers in all outerwear clothing."

"Huh?" His hands stilled and he glanced at her.

"It's not important." She pushed his hands away. "Here, I'll help."

"We need a pair of scissors." He peered down at the front of him. "Or maybe you can rip it."

12

She tugged, but it only drew the zipper tighter, making it catch more. Without anything to use, she leaned over and opened her mouth.

"Whoa … " Juan sank his hands into the hair piled on the top of her head. "I'd like nothing more, but having your mouth on me when you're upset probably isn't the smartest decision."

She paused with her opened mouth above the zipper and gazed up at him. "You don't want me to try and bite the string in half?"

He chuckled and patted her head before removing his hand and leaning back. "Be careful with those teeth, babe."

She lowered her head, caught the edge of the material, and ground her teeth back and forth. It was harder than she'd imagined. She grunted and worked the string over to her eyetooth.

The zipper grew taut and she reached up and tugged at the material. She stilled with her hand against his crotch. There was a reason for the lack of space between the fabric and the man. A very big reason.

Warmth flooded her face. Her skin tingled. The bulge underneath the pants fascinated, yet shocked her. A heady sensation, considering she could almost feel the heat radiating off him on her cheek.

The door opened and a flash went off in the room. She frowned at the same time the string gave way and she jerked away from Juan, spitting the remains of the thread off her lip. She stood and glanced behind her.

A robust, angry man in a coat with the USA Olympics emblem scrolled across the chest stood inside the doorway. Two photographers snapped pictures behind him, blinding Dana from inspecting them any further. Juan jumped off the table and stepped in front of her, blocking her from view.

"Oh, shit," Juan muttered.

"What are they doing?" she whispered, zipping Juan's coat to her neck. She wasn't sure if that helped, because on the bottom half, she still wore her thong and garter. "Who are they?"

Juan straightened, keeping his hand on her hip to keep her hidden behind his body. "It's not what it looked like, Coach Lindhurst."

"It was exactly what it looked like, and it'll be on the front cover of *Sports Illustrated* in the morning thanks to your carelessness. You were supposed to meet with the press a half-hour ago. Looks like that won't be necessary. They've got their pictures, and I imagine more than an article or two to fill the damn magazine, thanks to you and your entourage." Coach Lindhurst growled. "I've warned you. Your sponsor warned you. One more scandal and your benefactors would pull their money. I'm going to have to put you on reserve, dammit. You've really screwed up this time, Santiago."

Juan stepped forward, stopped, and glanced back at Dana. He gave her a hint of a smile before turning around. "Yes, Coach. If I could request another meeting, I can explain what happened here. It's a simple misunderstanding. One that shows that the lady behind me is innocent, and shouldn't be involved with any gossip that comes my way. She's had a bad day, sir."

Coach Lindhurst shook his head in disgust. "You had one more month to return and win another gold, and you threw it away because of some woman who wants a piece of—"

"Stop. Seriously, don't go there, or we're going to have problems between us. I'll talk to Wyden. I'll get my sponsor back," Juan said. "Can you keep me on the roster until then?"

"It's out of my hands. You had two warnings. Three marks and you're out. Balden will go in your place. You're immediately on reserve." Coach stared Juan down, cursed, and headed toward the door.

She scrambled out from behind Juan. "Wait!"

"What are you doing?" Juan whispered.

She ignored him, stepped over, and picked up her wedding dress, holding it in front of her. "Juan's right. There's a simple explanation for what you saw. You see, we're getting married. He was helping me into my dress, and I was helping him out of his suit. You can go to the lobby. There's a minister waiting for us. We're already late though, so if you'll excuse us, we need to finish getting dressed."

Juan walked over and ushered everyone out of the room, a look of bemusement on his face. Dana crossed her arms and cradled her elbows in her hand. It didn't take a genius to figure out Juan was on the Olympic team, and he was in deep trouble. She owed him for being so kind to her.

The more she thought about actually marrying him, the better she felt. She'd stay on her schedule, and figure out what to do later when she had time to think over her rash decision. She'd prove to Jace and her father that she was not spoiled. She'd help Juan for the goodness of the United States.

"Thanks, babe, but I can take it from here. This is my fault and I only have myself to blame." Juan ran his hands through his hair and groaned. "I'll figure out some way to make it back on the team with a new sponsor. This isn't the first time I've had to go in front of the board and prove myself to them."

She took off his coat and pushed it into his chest. "Get dressed."

"What?" He slipped his arms in the sleeves. "I said you could take the jacket. I've got plenty."

"We'll have to hurry or the minister will leave." She stepped into her dress and turned around. "Zip me up."

"You're not serious?"

She patted her hair. "I take it you need an excuse for what that man saw in here today to get back on the Olympic team, and I have a deadline. We're getting married."

"We can't." He tilted his head and looked up at the ceiling. "This is not happening to me."

"Yes, it is." She grabbed his hand. "I'm Dana Reese. My daddy is Colton Reese of Reese Enterprise. You know, the owner of the most popular line of ski equipment. He'll sponsor you, and be happy you took me off his hands. Trust me."

"Are you serious?"

"More than you'll ever know. I won't let Daddy or Jace ruin my life schedule." She laughed hysterically. "Let's go get married."

Chapter Two

Each of the Olympic panel members' voices echoed in Juan's head long after the meeting was over. He closed the sliding door of his suite and escaped to the balcony. The cold wind slapped him in the face, somewhat relieving the tension headache he'd developed when he'd said "I do" earlier to a woman he didn't know anything about—other than her name and the fact that her father owned the biggest ski equipment company in the world, and half the clothing factories in Europe that catered to winter-wear. He leaned over the railing, letting the snowflakes land on his overheated face.

One minute, Coach was putting him on reserve, stripping his chances of participating in the Olympics. The next minute, people were congratulating him on his nuptials and bolstering his drive to be a two-time gold medalist for the men's downhill ski team. With only one month to go, and twenty practices to keep himself in top shape, he needed to get his head in the sport.

He'd succeeded in straightening out his professional life, and jumped right into fucking up his personal life. He looked down at his left hand. The simple gold band constricted his finger. The piece of jewelry would throw off his grip on his poles, not to mention the odd feeling of having something foreign on his hand.

He felt like shit not having a ring for Dana, but he'd never planned to get married today.

Married?

He groaned. Buying a house in Tahoe, he could see himself doing. Hell, purchasing a yacht to cruise the isle with room for two or three women to sail with him, he'd do without thinking about it. But marriage?

Not for him. He wasn't sure if he'd ever find the one woman who'd make marriage worth it for him. Just thinking about spending more than a couple of days shut in a hotel room with only one woman gave him hives, and left him feeling guilty. His motto to spread himself around meant exactly that. And he sure didn't want to chain himself to a woman who loved someone else.

Marriage was a sacred union in his eyes. A one-time deal made with a woman who stole his heart and made him blind to everything else. He wasn't ready to settle down. His wife would be the one woman he spent the rest of his life with, and she'd have to be *the* one.

Even though Dana was the most beautiful woman he'd ever met, he knew nothing about her. Although, seeing her with her mouth going at his zipper earlier, he had an idea that he'd like to get to know her better.

She'd grabbed his attention when she ran past him in the lobby, almost knocking him against the wall in her hurry. The cream-colored lace dress hadn't registered. It was the way she'd hitched the hem to her thighs and ran, her shapely calves flashing him. Then he'd noticed the way her ass swished out of the room.

Any man would've noticed. It only made sense that he'd follow her and take another look. He'd expected to find a woman luring him to a private room. When she'd asked him to unzip her dress, well that was par for the course. That's what all females offered him. He could undress a sexy snow bunny in the dark with his eyes closed.

Married?

Hell, she'd thrust her hand out to shake his after the ceremony as if they'd agreed on a business deal instead of a life together. He ran his hands through his hair and groaned. She'd even turned her head when he'd leaned in for a kiss.

Not only had he gotten married. He'd hooked himself up with a sexy prude. What had he ever done to deserve that kind of punishment?

"Aw, shit." He straightened and shoved his hands in his coat pocket. "What do I do now?"

Tomorrow, his new married status would be plastered over every newspaper, in every sports magazine, and talked about on all the news channels. Juan Santiago, notable playboy and sexiest man in the upcoming Winter Olympics, veers off-course and head-banks on the rockiest course of his life. He'd be ruined.

Cold and miserable, he went back inside his suite and found Dana sitting on the edge of his couch. He walked to the other side of the room and sat on the love seat across from her. She'd changed clothes.

Skinny jeans, bunny boots, and the softest, tightest, palest pink, angora sweater hugged the plush curves he'd already seen earlier when she'd stripped down to barely anything. She'd let her hair down. Straight blonde streaks reached her elbows. His gut tightened, and his body betrayed him. He really did want to get to know her better—in a purely sexual way, of course.

"Daddy faxed the papers to the hotel. I picked them up in the office for you and set them on the table." She crossed her legs and slid her hands between her thighs. "He … uh … included a wedding present too, and his sponsorship papers are signed."

"Okay." Juan couldn't stop staring.

Dana darted her gaze from the floor to him to the door. He softened. Their rushed vows before the minister, the papers, the press conference, everything was finally catching up with them both. She was nervous and probably regretting her impulsive decision.

He stood. "There's a spare bedroom. If you tell me where to find your luggage, I'll get you settled in."

She sat forward. "Wait."

"Yeah?"

"I know this is weird." She scooted to the edge of the couch. "You needed help, and I … I need time to figure out a new schedule. But I'm feeling a little guilty. I mean, marriage? We don't even know each other."

"I know." He relaxed. "Me too."

"I work here, so I have my own room." Her smile didn't quite meet her eyes. "We can talk tomorrow when we're both thinking straight."

"You're not staying with me?"

She shook her head. "There's no reason to push myself on you further. Besides, I don't think your coach would want me causing you more stress. I get that you're the star of the team. Everyone in America is counting on you to bring home the gold."

Everything she said was true. Yet, she was his wife. Having her stay in her own room when he was responsible for her sat wrong with him.

In his family, marriage was forever. Guilt and disappointment in himself made the situation worse. Yet, it was obvious that she was alone. She'd had her world tipped upside down today. She shouldn't have to suffer alone.

"I only ski for two hours a day. Why don't you stay with me—in the spare room—and when we're both free, we can talk." He walked over, held out his hand, and smiled when she allowed him to pull her up from the couch. "You can go direct a bellhop to help bring your things to my ... our suite, and I'll order room service for dinner. I don't know about you, but getting married makes me hungry."

"You're being so cool about all this." Her shoulders sagged and she let her hair fall forward. She tossed her head in a perfect blend of flirtatious and feminine grace. "I promise. In a few days, I'll have an answer to both our problems. I'm good at figuring out solutions for tense situations. You'll see."

"I'm sure you'll figure it all out, babe." He gave her one of his killer smiles.

Her chin lifted. "And whatever happens, or whatever Daddy's papers say, I'll make sure he continues sponsoring you."

"We'll work it out. Don't worry. Go get your things brought to the suite, and I'll order dinner to come in an hour." He walked her to the door, put his hand low on her back, and encouraged her to leave.

He shut the door behind her, took two steps, and ripped off his coat and threw it with all his strength across the room. This called for some serious backup.

He pulled out his phone and called Crista Johnson, one of the few of his women friends that he could count on to be straight with him.

When Crista answered, he said, "Hey."

"You better have a good reason for calling me, Santiago," Crista said.

He laughed, relieved to catch her answering the phone. "Come on, sexy. I knew you were sitting by the phone hoping I'd call."

"I've been truly gifted." Crista snorted. "What kind of trouble have you gotten yourself into now?"

"Why would you ask that?"

"I know you." She sighed. "You seem to only call when you're having woman problems or you're in the hospital because you banged yourself up."

"That's not true," he muttered.

"Totally is, dude," she said. "Speak to me."

He closed his eyes for a beat. "I've totally screwed up."

"Let me decide that," she said gently. "Doesn't matter how big of problem you have, with your smooth moves, we can figure out a way to get you back on course."

"I got lowered to reserve."

"Dammit, Juan. You're almost on the plane to compete. We're not talking about rumor control or making up time on the slopes. This is serious. Have you been in front of the board yet?"

"I fixed that problem. I'm back on the roster." He paced the room. "There's more though, and it isn't pretty."

"You're worse than a girl. Get to the point. I'm about ready to call the airlines and go kick your butt myself," Crista said.

He stopped in front of the sliding door. "I got married."

Silence. If his news kept Crista from voicing her opinion, he was in deep shit.

"What do I do?" he asked.

"How the hell did you end up married?"

His chest tightened. "You know if I see a woman in need, I'm going to help. I thought she needed rescuing."

"Give me a break, Santiago. You saw your moment, and you took it. Women no longer need a man to save the day," Crista said.

"Our marriage was a spur of the moment decision for both of us. Trust me, pretending to be husband and wife will benefit me, and it'll be all over after the Olympics are done. It'll be like it never happened."

"Dick," Crista mumbled. "That's sick, Santiago. You can't mess with a woman's life like that. It's different for a man. You'll recover. She'll remember what happened to her for the rest of her life."

"I know," he said on a sigh. "I don't know what to do, except try to stay calm and wait until we can slip away quietly after the games and erase what we've done."

"Slap on your boxers and grow up. You're married, and now you have to deal with it." She paused. "I don't mean to add to your problems. I just didn't expect this. Married? I never thought you'd do it. Really, Juan, what were you thinking?"

He groaned. "I was thinking more along the lines of an annulment and hitting Friday night's Women Are Free down in the lounge. I'm not the marriage type of guy. I love women too much to settle down."

"What's your wife ... " she laughed loudly, "like?"

"She's hot. Blonde, stacked, legs that'd make any man hyperventilate. She's also smarter than the average snow bunny I go out with, which I'm finding incredibly sexy, and is leaving me more confused." He dropped his chin to his chest. "She's also a spoiled daddy's girl who can throw a tantrum and get whatever she wants. I doubt if she's had to work a day in her life for anything she's wanted. She just has to ask her father. Plus, she has some delusional thought process about life schedules that I really don't understand."

"I want to meet her," Crista said.

"Hell no. I'll be rid of her way before I see you again." He wiped his forehead. "Speaking of which, are you flying in to watch me?"

"Duh. Bruce and I expect to have front fence spots." She paused. "Listen, I gotta go. Someone's calling on the other line. I hope you figure out what to do, but you should give it some serious thought. There are worse things than being married, I've heard."

"I like my playboy status, Crista. I'm not ready to settle down. Someday, I'll marry the woman of my dreams because I love her beyond thinking, but right now? It's all about saving my career. You know me better than most people do, sweethcart. Thanks for listening to me complain. I'll talk to you later." He disconnected the call. A lot of help she was.

He turned and flinched. *Aw, hell.*

Dana stood in the open doorway, her luggage hanging from each hand. Shock, anger, and, if he wasn't mistaken, sadness showed in the pursed lips, the narrowed eyes, and the prudish stiffness of her body.

"How much did you hear?" he asked, slipping his hands into the front pockets of his jeans.

"Enough to understand what you think about me." She dropped the bags in the doorway, pivoted, and disappeared down the hallway.

Great. Married an hour and he'd already managed to piss off his wife. Could today get any worse?

Chapter Three

How could she have thought Juan was nice? Dana walked back in the direction of her room. In the elevator it dawned on her, she couldn't hide away because she'd turned her room key into Sarah at the front desk.

She'd lived at the hotel for two months, and still had one month to go before she pulled up shop and headed home to Colorado for a break. She enjoyed being the Reese distributor and saleswoman during the winter months at different ski resorts. It beat working alongside her dad at the main office.

Now she was married. What a mistake.

She pushed the first floor button. Too bad she couldn't fly back to daddy's house and hide out there while the family was gone. But she'd already told her father she was skipping any kind of honeymoon, so now she had to work all next week. The doors slid open. She walked out and headed toward the lounge.

Settled in the back corner, near the floor to ceiling windows overlooking the lit snow covered slopes, she gulped down half of the double martini she'd ordered before she slowed down to pace herself. She'd only been trying to find a way out of her troubles—so how had she managed to dig herself into an even bigger hole?

Juan seemed to be feeling similarly. For all his attitude and convincing speech that everything would work out in the end, he'd talked down about her to another woman. For all she knew, the woman on the phone was a long-term girlfriend or one of his girls at another lodge. Well, Dana wasn't one of his admirers. Thank you very much.

Disgusted by her behavior, she picked up her phone and dialed her father. She hated admitting defeat and needing his help, but she had a feeling she'd need his lawyer to get herself out of her marriage.

"Dana?" Her father spoke to someone in the background, and then continued. "What's wrong now?"

"I need you to contact John Blate," she said.

"My attorney?"

"Yeah." She sank further down in the chair. "I might've made a mistake in marrying—"

"Juan Santiago," her father bellowed. "Probably the one thing you've done right, dammit."

She grimaced. "No, I really think—"

"You need time, especially with a man like Santiago." Her dad sighed heavily. "Once you've calmed down, we'll talk. If you still think you need to get out of your marriage, I'll hire one of the best divorce lawyers in the state. Just think about what you're doing and to whom you're married before making a rash decision. Your union with him could skyrocket sales for the company."

"But, I—"

"You've always been impulsive," her dad said. "Listen to me for once. Your marriage is exactly what we ... uh ... you needed."

"Whatever," she muttered. "I need to go. I'll call you in a couple of days."

She disconnected the call and stared at the phone. Without hesitating, she brought up the browser on the screen and searched her husband's name. Watch it turn out that he was already married to that Crista woman he was talking to on the phone, and now she'd broken the law. It was one thing to marry on a whim, but she was a Reese. Scandal was something she didn't do.

Daddy would kill her if she brought any more disappointment down on the family. She'd already put herself on his bad side by defending her right to work at the rental shop at the lodge and refusing to jump into the shark pool of sellers. She enjoyed doing the same thing day after day without anyone knowing where she came from or who her father was.

But there was something in her father's tone of voice that told her she was missing some important detail. He seemed too excited, too happy, too encouraging about her marriage to Juan.

A Santiago fan site popped on screen. She scanned the headings. *Oh. My. God.*

Not only had she married a member of the U.S. Olympic men's ski team, but also the guy everyone nicknamed Amante Español. She traced her finger over his face. *Spanish Lover.*

How could she not have connected that the man known for seducing women in every city was the same guy who'd helped her strip out of her clothes?

He'd romanced and flirted his way across the world, and no woman had ever tied him down. She shut off her phone. Now she remembered what she'd heard about Juan's background. Known as the kid who'd worked his way up from poverty to a millionaire, charming everyone on and off the slopes, he was also the sports world's most eligible bachelor, according to *People* magazine. Her daddy's fortunes wouldn't impress someone who'd built their own success.

She smacked the top of the table. That's why her dad wanted her to stay married to Juan. A famous skier would bring more attention to Reese Enterprise, which meant more money coming in to the company and her father's hands.

But that didn't explain why Juan married her.

A squeal and loud cheering broke out across the lounge, interrupting her thoughts. She gazed at the bar, spotted Juan surrounded by his fans, and slouched further down in the chair. He'd followed her.

Along with a dozen women, he stood in the lounge, smiling at everyone as if his life hadn't changed at all a few hours ago when he said *I do*. She drained the rest of her drink. No one, not even Amante Español, would make a fool out of her.

She stood, shoved her phone in her pocket, and worked her way around the empty tables to her husband. Standing behind him, she overhead more than she wanted to hear.

"Thank you, sweetheart. Not tonight. I've got practice in the morning, and need to be alert and ready to ski my heart out." He accepted the exuberant hug from a woman with bleach blonde hair and fake boobs.

Another woman, taller and dressed more for a summer night's party than the winter season pushed her way between Dane and Juan. "I'll make it worth your time, and leave you more energetic. The things I can do for you, no woman will be able to match, Juan."

Seriously? What a conceited bitch. Dana reached between them and yanked the woman away. "You're more than anyone can handle, honey. Go sink your claws into someone else's husband."

The woman topped Dana's own five-foot-five body by a good four inches, but Dana refused to back down when the woman got in her face. Geez, what did Juan see in these skanky girls?

"Babe." Juan slipped his arm across her shoulders and led her away from the group. "I was looking for you. You shouldn't have run off."

"Don't 'babe' me." She glared without missing a step. "New rule. While our marriage is still valid, you won't embarrass me by hanging around your groupies."

"What?" He laughed. "My groupies?"

"Sluts, hos, bunnies, skanks, bitches," she waved her hand, "whatever you call them. I'm trying to be considerate, since you obviously have some reason why you married me when you're rolling in money and can save your own ass."

"You threw yourself at my mercy. You didn't have to say *I do.*" His mouth hardened and he dropped his arm. "And I can't finance my way into the Olympics—it looks bad and my fans need to see that I have sponsors who believe in me enough to put their name on my back."

"Whatever." She stormed off in front of him and entered the elevator. When the door closed, she turned to him. "I am a Reese. I will not allow you to embarrass, ruin, or damage my family's name. Until I can talk to my lawyer in the morning, stay away from other women ... and me."

"A lawyer?" He frowned. "Now, wait a damn minute."

"I'm sure he can have our marriage annulled by the end of the week." She exited the elevator.

He caught up with her and flashed a smile that made her catch her breath. "What's the hurry? I thought we had an agreement."

"I'm sure you want to get back to Crista and your thousands of women who are ready to show you the art of screwing while standing on their head."

"Where did you get that number?" He threw back his head and laughed.

"I Googled you." She crossed her arms. "It was rather enlightening in a gross, rather pathetic way if you're big on making your mark on the world by how many pants you've ripped off willing women."

"Don't believe everything you read or hear," he muttered.

"You're telling me that those women out there" she pointed at the door, "are not the same ones who I've spotted coming off this floor with their bare asses jiggling early in the morning when I'm going downstairs to work. I don't know, Juan, they sure look familiar. I know a pleased smile when I see one."

"No doubt they're the same ones." He sat on the couch and stretched out. "But I'm telling you, I haven't slept with any of them. You'll just have to believe me."

She snorted.

"I'm serious. It's been two months since I've had sex."

"Setting world records there, *Amante Español*." She rolled her eyes, unable to keep the sarcasm out of her voice.

He grinned. "Vicious, babe."

"Will you stop smiling? It's disturbing. There's nothing funny about our situation."

"I like this side of you," he said.

"You mean for a spoiled daddy's girl, I'm two dimensional?" she said through clenched teeth.

"Shit." He groaned. "I didn't mean that, babe."

"Yes, you did. I heard you."

"No." He stood. "Okay, I did mean that, but not in a bad way. In a month, competitions will start and once I'm done, we'll go our separate ways. Until then, can you act like you enjoy being married to me?"

One month. She stared at Juan. If it would keep her in her daddy's good graces a little longer until she had her life on track, maybe. At least a month would buy her enough time to find the strength inside of her to continue with her plans with a new direction.

She stuck out her hand. "Fine. I'll wait a month, but you can't hook up with any other women while we're married. That's embarrassing for me, and I don't want anyone laughing behind my back."

"No problem, babe. You won't regret it. I promise." He ignored her offer of a handshake and cupped her face with his hands.

"W-what are you doing?" she whispered.

"It's called a kiss to seal the deal." He lowered his head.

His breath fed her. In. Out. One more inch and their lips would touch.

"That's n-not a good idea." She stared into his eyes, which resembled melted chocolate right before it started to boil.

He titled his head. "It's a very good beginning … "

His gaze went to her mouth and his lashes covered his eyes. She moistened her lips. What would he taste like?

She grasped his shirt, unsure whether she wanted to push him away or pull him closer. "With a quick ending."

"Stop talking," he murmured, tilting her face higher.

"I'm afraid to."

"Why?"

Her breath caught. "You might ki—"

His mouth captured hers. A light kiss that allowed her time to adjust to the reality that she was kissing the famous Amante Español.

The kiss was warm and firm, but soft enough to make her want more. She leaned in slightly, and electricity shot through her. Need burned hot and bright, melting her resolve not to ever touch him. *Oh, God, I'm in trouble.*

He let go of her face and cupped the back of her head, holding her in place, while his free hand went to her lower spine and tugged her closer. He used just enough pressure to draw her that much more intimately against him, but not make her feel confined or forced.

Parts of her began to ache. Startled, she realized she'd never felt this way with Jace.

Juan deepened the kiss, then pulled back and looked into her eyes. "There will be more kissing."

She nodded, before she caught herself. "I mean, no. We can't do that again."

Aware of how dangerous being married to America's playboy was, she escaped to her room and shut the door. For good measure, she turned the lock. Her knees shook and her heart raced, and she knew it wasn't fear, but an uncontrollable lust for her new husband that had her hiding.

Chapter Four

Snow blew sideways on the north slope of the mountain. Juan stood at the top of the run and adjusted his goggles. Last trip down for the day, and all he could think about was how Dana's lips had softened against his last night.

Despite his distraction during practice thinking about his *wife*, he'd clocked in on his second run. The coach was happy, and his wife's daddy was footing the bill for him to continue skiing. He gripped the poles. As soon as the Olympics came and went, he'd pay back his new father-in-law.

Being related to his sponsor sat wrong with him, and the guilt by association troubled his sleep. He pushed off the slope, leaning low and gaining speed. No one paid his way because of a deal made on his behalf.

The fact that the money came for marrying Dana felt too much like a payoff for him to be comfortable with the arrangement. He stabbed the ground with the end of his pole, shifted, and pushed off. He used the powder to gain speed. What kind of father paid someone to take his daughter off his hands?

Snow clung to his goggles. He ignored the harsh conditions affecting his visibility. Trees were on his left, and the chair line was on the right. He could close his eyes and know the trail without spotting the land markers.

A burst of speed pushed him to the last crossover, and he put his skis together and rode to the finish line. Cheers from the fans gathered behind the fenced area knocked his wayward thoughts of how his life sucked at this moment away. He skied his way to the barrier.

He'd never forget where he came from and where he was now. His fans came first, because they'd gotten him this far. Without their dedication, their hope of him succeeding, pushing him forward to be the best, he'd be just another guy wearing a pair of skis. They made him the athlete that he'd become. He never wanted to disappoint them.

He pushed his goggles over his stocking hat and smiled. "Hey, ladies ... "

Camera flashes blinded him. He held out his hand and moved along the fence. There was no reason to see their faces. All his fans expected the same thing, whether they were single, married, divorced, female or male. He acknowledged them all, gave them a little more of himself that they could take away with them and in the end, he was left alone, unsettled and missing a true relationship.

His real fans were sitting in classrooms, dreaming about someday winning their own gold, or at home watching television, cheering him on. It was the people who he'd never know or meet that inspired him. It all came back to the start, because he was the kid who'd sat at home, staring at the flight of the professional skier, dreaming of the day he would be old enough to be that famous, that good, that much of an idol.

"Thank you." He raised his hand, pushing away. "Everyone ready to cheer on the U.S.A.?"

"U.S.A., U.S.A., U.S.A.," the crowd chanted.

He waved, holding up one finger to show he'd earn the number one spot. Then he turned and skied toward the lodge. He had the rest of the day off, and a soak in the hot tub sounded better than winning the Olympics right now. His shoulder ached, and he knew the tension he was under wasn't helping anything.

Even though the time clock put him right on target today, he'd felt stiff on the turns and had put too much distance behind his strokes. He spotted a crowd at the back door to the lodge and skied faster. Normally, he snuck inside past the retailers during the day to escape the guests staying at the lodge for the season, but the crowd gathered around the door would make that impossible today.

He skidded to a stop. The group was too large for him to see what was drawing everyone's attention. He nudged the guy in front of him. "What's happening?"

"The chick in one of the booths kicked everyone out." The man shrugged. "I'm buying a new pair of gloves, so I hope she opens up soon."

A sinking feeling came over Juan. "What's the woman look like?"

The man raised his brows. "A real looker. She's the reason why I came down to buy the gloves. It's not as if I need a new pair, if you know what I mean."

Juan exhaled. "What color hair?"

"Blonde," the man said.

Juan clicked off his skis, picked them up, and pushed his way through the crowd, excusing himself the whole way. At the back door, he stopped in front of an angry woman with gorgeous blonde hair who glared at him. Moreover, his wife's displeasure seemed personal.

He widened his stance, blocking the others from view. "Hey, what's up, babe?"

"Don't 'babe' me," she whispered harshly. "This is all your fault."

"What did I do?" he said.

"As if you don't know." She leaned forward, until the top of her head was level with his chin. "Kiss me, dammit."

He chuckled and meant to step back, more amused than concerned, but she grabbed his jacket and pulled him toward her. Their lips collided, and he winced. She definitely had a temper.

When she continued to press her pursed lips against him, he dropped the skis and took her in his arms. If she wanted to kiss in front of the crowd, he wouldn't turn her down. But he wasn't going to let her bruise her lips to prove a point.

He cupped the back of her head, cradling her in his hand, and leaned her backward. Her mouth opened in surprise, and he took control of the kiss. A real kiss, not some assault.

He enveloped her bottom lip, then moved to capture both before pulling away slightly and then diving back in. His soul smiled when her mouth softened and her neck arched. He held her in place, tilting his head, wanting to revisit the taste that had driven him crazy last night. All he could come up with was she reminded him of a cool breeze coming off the ocean on a summer day.

Rejuvenating.

Tempting.

Exhilarating.

He swept his tongue along hers until her fingers dug through his insulated jacket to his arm. Only when he supported her full weight did he straighten and pull away from her lips without letting her go.

Dana stared drunkenly up at him. Her gaze no longer shot daggers, but had gone all soft and dreamy. He leaned back down.

"How about we unlock the door and let the guests inside," he whispered into her ear.

She nodded, but otherwise made no move to address the people waiting behind them. He slipped his hand into her coat pocket. Empty.

Juan kissed her lightly, switched his holding arm, and dug into her other pocket. His fingers curled around the set of keys. Sweeping up her hand, he walked her to the door while he fiddled with the keys.

When he found the right one and opened the back door of the lodge, his wife still hadn't snapped out of the kiss, so he pulled her to the side to make way for the people hurrying inside the building. He nodded and smiled at the curious looks and blatant snickering.

Once the last person left him alone with Dana, he turned and slipped his hand behind Dana's neck. He wanted another taste.

"Get your hands off me," she said, jerking away from him.

"Whoa … " He raised his hands. "You asked me to kiss you. Babe, you were right there kissing me back and liking it."

"So?" she mumbled, pacing in front of him.

He was missing something. "You enjoyed it a lot."

"Shh." She swiped the air with her arm, cutting him off. "That's not important."

The hell it wasn't. He gazed out at the ski slope, running back through the last five minutes and trying to understand what was going on. He was clueless. The only thing he knew was that Dana loved to pace. She paced any time she was angry, nervous, or confused.

"I can't do this." She stopped walking, and planted her hands on her hips. "It's over."

"What's over?" he asked.

She frowned. "Us. You and me. Our marriage."

Shit. Something big did happen?

"Talk to me." He stepped forward.

She stiffened, lifting her chin. He ignored her attempts to push him away. She was talking about ruining everything. He wasn't asking for a lifetime. He only needed her to pretend to be his loving wife for four weeks.

"Everyone is laughing at me." She rubbed her lips together and looked beyond him. "Four people this morning informed me that our marriage is a joke, including one of your teammates."

He brushed her hair back from her cheek. "Who?"

"Curt Balden." She glared at him. "Not only him, but probably every woman you've slept with since arriving at the lodge. Trust me. They're not shy about alluding to the fact that our marriage is a sham, and you'll never settle for one woman. Curt told me that he bet another teammate a thousand dollars that you'd dump me within a week. Do you realize how that makes me feel, because I know you don't want to be married to me?"

"Wait a minute, I—"

"Stop." She shook her head. "I don't want to hear anything you have to say. I need to fix my life and get back on schedule. I can't have everyone talking about me."

"I agree." He picked up his skis. "I'll take care of it. No one will say another word to you about our relationship."

Dana hurried to keep up with him as he walked toward the lodge. "You're going to fix this?"

"Yeah." He held the door open for her. "You're my wife."

She moved around him and planted her hands on his chest. "Wait. You can't act all macho and expect me to trust you."

"Yes, I can." He inhaled deeply and relaxed. "I know this isn't easy for you, but no one—not my fans, my teammates, or your father—are allowed to upset *my* wife. Got it?"

Her mouth formed a perfect O. He grinned. She flipped emotions faster than the weather, and he had to admit, he liked that. She kept things interesting.

One to always push his luck, he decided to go for the finish line. "When do you get off work?"

"In two hours," she said.

He peered over at the clothing shop, packed with customers. "I'm going to host a hot tub party at the room and invite a few of the guys over."

"Oh," she said. "I'll hang out in the lounge and … "

He lifted her chin. "I want you there with me. Once the team accepts you, everyone else will too. You'll see. Just relax, and be yourself."

She raked her teeth over her bottom lip. "Okay, but no more kissing me."

He chuckled. "You kissed me first, remember?"

"I thought it would show everyone that our marriage was real, I didn't mean anything by it. You're the one who actually kissed me back. You were supposed to keep your mouth closed." Her gaze dropped to his lips.

"How about we go with the flow? If we're getting along and I kiss you, you let me," he whispered. "I mean, we wouldn't want to argue in front of my friends, right? That's what this is all about … proving our marriage is real and saving face."

"Okay," she said.

He swallowed. "Good."

She backed away. "No tongue though."

"Whatever you want, babe," he said.

"And no calling me babe." She whirled around and hurried to the shop.

He stood watching her retreat. Damn, his wife had a tight ass. She had no idea how much he loved a challenge, and he looked forward to making her change her mind.

Along with the surprise of how much he wanted Dana, he had to admit he'd pegged her wrong. He had no idea why Colton Reese's daughter wasn't sunning it up in some resort half way across the world, and instead was the distributor and saleswoman at the lodge. That wasn't a sign of a spoiled lady. She was hardworking and from what he could see, she wasn't afraid of putting in time to make an honest living for herself.

Chapter Five

Juan sat on the edge of the hot tub, directly behind Dana, his bare legs pressed against her shoulders, cradling her between his legs. The hot water she was sitting in paled to the heat coming off Juan's body. Every so often, he'd brush her wet hair off her forehead, her back, her neck. His hand hadn't left some part of her body for the last twenty minutes.

As she'd finished with her work for the day, she'd grown angrier at Juan's attempt to undermine her authority. He couldn't tell her how they were going to run their faux marriage. He'd distracted her from her main goal of organizing her shambles of a life.

But from the moment she'd walked out of her room in the bikini, determined to show him what he couldn't have, he'd acted all dominating and possessive. He hadn't let her out of his sight all night. Nor would he allow any of the men within arm's reach of her. If her back weren't turned toward him, she'd nail him with a go-to-hell glare, but there was no easy way to deflect his attention without causing a scene.

Damn him.

Even now, his hands were doing delicious things to the back of her neck. Not to be sidetracked by her husband, she said, "So, Curt, how do you manage your schedule—all the practices, real life activities—and still call Boulder your home?"

"I'd have to ask my manager." Curt laughed. "He tells me what to do and where to go, and how to handle everything."

Dana sighed. The shaggy blond hair and quick dimple impressed other women, or so she'd heard during the season, but the dude wouldn't be able to make his own breakfast if left on his own. How was she going to learn anything about approaching sales outlets about a new product if she only hung around jocks?

Travis Darrow flung his arms to the side and pulled himself out of the water. Lanky and tall for a skier, he was the quietest out of the four men who'd joined Juan and her tonight. Joe Bloom, a huge flirt who hadn't stopped winking at her, and T.T. Tibens, who'd disappeared ten minutes ago to grab something to eat out of the fridge, completed their little party. Not that she'd call sitting in hot water being stared at all that exciting.

"So, how did you guys meet?" Joe winked at Juan.

Okay, maybe Joe had a tick and he wasn't putting the moves on her.

She relaxed. "We met—"

"Months ago." Juan put both of his hands on her shoulders and massaged her muscles. "That's the reason I've been so distracted this season. I couldn't stand to be away from her, so when she talked her dad into letting her run his shop at the lodge, my life straightened out. I finally had her to myself. We were going to wait until after the Olympics to get married, but love comes first. My girl is the most important thing to me. I wanted to make it permanent—" his hands stilled on her "—and yesterday, we made it official."

She leaned her head against the inside of his thigh, wishing his story was true and knowing their fake relationship was anything but the forever kind. "Lucky for us there was a preacher in the lodge, and we were able to say our 'I dos.' Now we need to concentrate on Juan winning the gold."

Before she could smile to cover their story, Juan tipped her head back and kissed the end of her nose. Her nose!

"Forever, baby," he whispered.

She ducked her chin, and between the heat of the water and Juan, she boiled. "Let me change positions with you, honey. I'm getting too warm."

The other guys laughed for some reason. She quickly swiveled around, took Juan's hands, and pulled herself out of the tub. How Juan manipulated her, she had no idea, but there she was, sitting in the exact spot he'd vacated with her legs wide open, and his head leaning back against her stomach.

Oh my God ...

She flailed her hands in the air, not knowing where to put them. Catching a glimpse of his teammates watching her, she did the only thing she could think of, and put her hands on Juan's shoulders. Surprisingly, she calmed down.

She wanted to blame her reaction on Juan being the only person here she semi-knew, but she'd be lying. Her husband fascinated her in a good way. He tempted her to forget they were playing and that their marriage was a sham.

T.T. came out the sliding door. "Looks like Amante Español has officially retired. Man, I'll miss all the women he cast off to me."

Dana jolted at hearing Juan's nickname. His reputation reflected back at her. If there was one thing she'd learned being raised by her father it was that you don't sully the family name.

"That name is buried and dead." Juan looped his arms over Dana's thighs. "You know how I hated the press calling me the Spanish Lover. It's bad enough I'm the only Hispanic skiing for the U.S. team, I don't need the added reputation."

Dana bit the inside of her cheek. She had a feeling he wasn't putting on a show for the guys. He really did dislike the name the press picked for him.

Curious about what kinds of pre-disposed battles he'd fought to make his way to the top, she couldn't help opening her mouth. "Well, I can be the first one to tell everyone that skiing is your life. I've never met a more dedicated, hard-working person in my life."

Juan turned his head and kissed the inside of her thigh. She stroked his hair. She'd spoken the truth. He was professional and honest. The fans loved him and he'd saved her ass. He'd set her life schedule back on the right path ... momentarily.

"Damn, man, you have me missing my woman." Travis jumped out of the hot tub. "I'll be back."

"Where's he going?" T.T. asked after the door slid closed.

Joe chuckled. "Ten bucks says he's going to call Stephanie."

"Who's she?" Dana said.

Juan tilted his head back. "His girl. They've been going out for about a year. Stephanie's on the U.S. gymnastic team."

"Stephanie Hyatt?" Dana's mouth came open when Juan nodded. "Oh my God, I love her. She's America's sweetheart. I cheered for her after she sprained her ankle on her dismount during the last games."

"That's her," Juan said.

"Wow." She gazed at the door. "Stephanie and Travis." She shook her head. "He's so shy, and she loves the camera. I never would've guessed."

"Opposites attract," T.T. mumbled.

Juan shifted and rubbed his shoulder. Dana frowned. She'd noticed him massaging his arm earlier.

She leaned over and whispered, "Are you okay?"

"Yeah, I'm fine." He stood. "I'm about done in, guys. I think we're going to call it a night."

Dana planted her feet on the deck, and stood. She grabbed two towels, and handed one to Juan before wrapping the other one around herself. She was glad he'd put an end to their party. She had a gazillion questions for him.

Then minutes later, Dana and Juan stood in the living room alone. She crossed her arms, holding the towel on her.

"I'm going to take a shower," Juan said.

"Me too." She moved to go to her own room and collided into his side. "Sorry."

He steadied her. "Dana, I ... "

She gazed up into his eyes. Her chest tightened, and she had a fleeting thought that she'd disappointed him somehow. It left her uneasy. "Is something wrong?"

Maybe he'd changed his mind. The charade had to be harder on him because he spent all his time surrounded by his team, his friends. He'd lied about their situation, and from what she'd learned, he usually told the truth.

He shook his head. "No. Everything's good. I only wanted to see if you'd like to watch a movie or something. It's still early."

"Oh, okay. Sure." She moved away from him. "That sounds nice."

She turned and hurried into her bedroom and slammed the door. Her heart raced erratically, and she pressed her hand to her forehead. What was she doing?

She couldn't jump every time Juan came within a foot of her. She sagged against the door, and then slapped her hand over her mouth. *Oh my God.*

Did he just ask her out on a date to watch a movie in their hotel room?

Chapter Six

If anyone asked her the name of the movie playing on the television, Dana wouldn't have a clue. She pulled her feet up onto the couch and tucked the blanket around her legs. Once Juan had started answering her questions, he'd focused entirely on her.

The movie was only background noise.

"What's your mom's name?" Dana asked.

"Ana." Juan's mouth softened. "God, I'd give anything to eat one of her dinners. I miss her cooking. When Mom and my sister, Maria, get together, we eat for days. They cook enough to feed the whole neighborhood. It's always a good thing when I go back into season, because I always gain at least ten pounds when I'm home in Oregon. They only live a few miles away from me and bring me leftovers all the time."

His whole demeanor changed when he talked about his family. Dana smiled, happy that he had his memories to hold him while he was away from home and on the road. Instead of making her feel jealous of where he came from, or sad about the obvious lack of comforting memories in her own life, his stories simply fascinated her.

Her own upbringing had involved visits between her divorced parents, and court cases while they hashed out their dislike of one another in front of a judge. Family usually wasn't a topic she wanted to talk about with others, but hearing about the love Juan had for his mom and sister was like listening to a bedtime story.

"Pancakes or waffles?" she asked.

His brow wrinkled. "Waffles."

"Me too. I love how the holes collect the butter so it doesn't run off." She tapped her lips with her finger until Juan's gaze grew intense, and she quickly said, "Favorite color?"

"Blue," he said.

"Brunettes, blondes, or redheads?" Heat rushed to her neck.

Not that she was curious. It was a normal question. Everyone had a preference.

"Blondes with blue eyes." His voice lowered. "You set me up."

She laughed. "Yeah, I totally did."

But his answer pleased her, even if he was protecting himself and answering her the way she wanted him to. He was smooth. He probably dodged questions from the press all the time and answered depending on what he knew they'd want to hear.

"How about you?" He glanced at her and flashed a smile. "What kind of guy do you go for?"

She flipped her hair. "Once I met the man they call Amante Español, no other man would compare."

Juan stared at her, and then opened his mouth and laughed. Her stomach flip-flopped, and although they were teasing each other, the sight of him letting the stress of their situation go delighted her. She rather liked the person he was when they were alone and not worrying about tomorrow.

"I never thought to ask you, but am I trespassing on someone else's property?" She caught her lip between her teeth.

"Huh?" Juan crossed his ankles.

She wrinkled her nose. "We kind of flew right into marriage and I have no idea if I've ticked some other woman off. Maybe a girlfriend back home? I mean, I know the other women are mad at me ... I've heard the talk, and they're not shy about letting me know I won't keep you. But I need to know—"

"There's no girlfriend and despite what you've been told, there's no woman in my life." He raised his brow. "Okay?"

She nodded, and relaxed. "Just so you know, I don't have any more fiancés waiting to dump me hanging in the background either. Well, except for you, but you're my husband. That's totally different. You can't really get rid of me now without a … you know … " she gulped, damning her big mouth, "divorce."

"An annulment," he muttered. "This isn't real."

"Right," she said.

She wasn't going to let that fact bother her. She plucked a piece of fuzz off the flannel blanket. Tomorrow, she'd call Daddy's attorney and find out what would have to be done next month after their marriage of convenience was completed.

"So, what's your chance of winning the gold?" She pushed past the melancholy thoughts.

Juan grinned. "Do you really care?"

She scoffed. "Seriously, dude? You have to ask?"

He raised he brows. "Dude?"

"Yeah. We're past the first name basis … you're a dude." She grinned. "Give me the scoop. Who do you have to beat?"

"Bannister from Denmark. He's fast, experienced, and I outweigh him by fifteen pounds." Juan's gaze landed on the floor. "I'm coming back from an injury, so I'm not sure what this year will be like for me."

"What?" She rose up on her knees on the couch. "Where?"

He rubbed his shoulder. "Rotary cuff. Right here. I lost two months of practice over the summer. Precious time I needed to nail my times. As it is, I'm skiing at about eighty percent."

"What's that mean?" she asked.

"I'm missing my times twenty percent of the time. You're only given so many runs, and each one counts. I screw up on one, and I can kiss the gold goodbye." He grimaced. "Just between you and me, I don't feel right, despite the doctor giving me the okay. I don't know if I'm babying that side of me, or if I've lost the range of motion I had before the injury. Although all my tests check out."

"Is there anything I can do?" she asked.

He shook his head. "Thanks, but no. I'm hoping I can work through whatever it is. It's probably mental, and will go away once the pressure is on. We'll be in Germany soon."

"We?" she said.

He nodded. "You'll go too. You're my wife."

"When are we going?" she asked.

"Three weeks."

"Oh, God." She threw off her blanket. "Give me your phone."

He shifted to his hip, removed his cell from his back pocket, and handed it to her. She punched at the keypad and waited. Finally, her call was answered.

"Dad, I need my passport. I don't even know if it's valid anymore and I need it to go with Juan to Germany." She rolled her eyes at Juan. "No, I don't have time to do it myself."

Juan waved his hand. "Dana. I can—"

She stuck her finger in front of his face. "Yes. Just have her send it to the hotel. Thank you, Daddy."

She returned Juan's phone to him. "Daddy will get my passport to me. I forgot all about needing it. Actually, I never thought you'd take me to Germany, but I'm excited. I've never been to the Olympics. I wonder what the opening ceremony will be like?"

"Hang on a minute, babe. Let's get something straight first." He scooted back on the couch. "We're married."

She nodded. "I know that. I won't tell anyone differently."

"Okay. You're not getting me." He tightened his lips over his teeth. "I'm your husband."

"Duh." She laughed.

"New rule. You don't run to your dad every time you need something. That's my job." He kicked off his sneakers.

"But he does all the important things for me. You don't understand our relationship. He believes I'm incapable of running my own life, and I like it that way. Granted, I push him away, but if I don't ask him to do the little things, he'll realize I'm

46

more valuable than he thinks I am right now, and he'll put more demands on me to stay in the company. As it is, if I let him think I'm incompetent, it … well, it buys me more time to plan my life without his interference." She sank back into the corner of the couch. "You'd have to know him to understand our screwed up relationship. Trust me."

"Maybe, but as a man, I won't have my girl asking her father for help. That's my job, and for you to go behind my back makes me appear weak and without the balls to stand up to my wife." He pinned her with a look. "I have balls."

She snorted. "You're very chivalrous, aren't you?"

"There's nothing wrong with wanting to take care of the woman I care about," he said.

She swallowed. "But we're only pretending to be married."

Juan studied her without answering. She dropped her gaze, grabbing the ends of her hair and separating them into individual strands. *If* they were married, she'd want her husband to help her. *If* they loved each other, she'd want to do as much for him as he did for her. *If* they … she tossed her hair over her shoulder.

"Okay. I'll come to you first when I have a problem," she said.

His eyes softened, and he remained silent. He gave his acceptance without rubbing it in her face that she let him have his way. Warmth filled her and she shared a grin with Juan. Not once in her life had she ever received such quiet approval. She'd always had to guess if Jace was truly happy with her, because he neither showed nor told her what he was feeling. The lack of communication drove her nuts, but she'd convinced herself it was for the best. Usually, she worked her butt off trying to please everyone, and fell short.

With Jace, she pretended his coldness meant she was pleasing him. At least he wasn't trying to change her. Juan's obvious approval made her feel good about herself and she wanted to continue putting that look on his face, so he'd continue to be happy with her.

"I know about your dad ... what about your mom?" Juan stretched his legs out in front of him and laid his head on the back of the couch.

Dana picked at the edge of the blanket. "I haven't seen her since I was sixteen and moved in permanently with my dad. Our relationship had always been strained, even before that, but she viewed my decision to live with Dad as a betrayal of sorts, I guess. Phone calls dwindled, and now we call each other on Christmas."

"I'm sorry," he mumbled.

She shrugged. "It is what it is. I've come to realize I can't take responsibility for how my parents act."

Juan laid his hand over her fingers, stilling their movement. "No brothers or sisters?"

She smiled. "Three stepbrothers from my dad's fourth wife. Aaron is ten, Max is twelve, and Jonathon is sixteen. They make dealing with my dad worth every minute."

"You love them," he whispered.

She nodded. "Yeah. It's weird, because I never grew up having to deal with siblings, but I love the times I'm asked to take care of them while my dad and their mom travel. They're great boys. Aaron and Max are big into video games, and Jonathon is into my car. He recently got his driver's license, so you can see why he likes staying with me in Colorado."

Juan continued holding her hand. "Let me guess ... a Porsche?"

She shook her head. "Of course not."

He rolled his head against the couch and gazed up at the ceiling. "BMW?"

"No." She laughed. "Really, do I look like a snob?"

He pulled her hand, and she tumbled across the couch until she laid her head in his lap. Her breath whooshed out of her. Sitting beside him on the couch, she could handle. The hot tub seating arrangement, she'd conquered, although she enjoyed it way too much. But lying on Juan's lap made formulating any sort of thought impossible.

"Only when wearing someone else's wedding dress," he whispered.

She blinked. "What?"

"When I saw you the first time, I took you for a snob. You were throwing a fit about your canceled wedding and demanding your daddy fix your life." He cupped her cheek, holding her from turning away from him. "I assumed you were spoiled rotten."

"I'm not," she whispered.

"I can see that," he whispered back.

She closed her eyes for a moment before looking at him again. "I might be a little high-strung though."

He grinned. "Yeah, a little."

"And my Jaguar is sweet," she added.

The corner of his eyes crinkled and he whispered, "I bet it is."

She lay there thinking over the turn of events the last twenty-four hours. She'd gone from one wild idea to the next, but tonight, the clock stopped. It was just she and Juan. There was no mention of their plan on how to go forward.

If she closed her eyes—and she did—she could imagine this was real. They got along rather well, and conversation flowed evenly between them. She sighed. There was no denying she was attracted to him.

His kisses stayed on her mind throughout the day. Never had a man held her so tenderly while making her feel consumed. Defenseless to stop him—not that she wanted to—she'd surrendered to him willingly.

She yawned and snuggled deeper under the blanket that moved over her shoulders. Juan covered her, but she was too tired to tell him thank you.

He put his hand on her head and stroked her hair. He really was attentive.

Chapter Seven

Juan's legs were numb. He shifted out from underneath Dana and stood, flexing his muscles. The prickles disappeared as his circulation came back and he gazed down at her. She'd fallen asleep on his lap last night and soon after, he'd closed his eyes too.

Despite the awkward position and the less than comfortable couch, he'd slept all the way through the night. He couldn't remember the last time he'd felt so rested.

Dana surprised the hell out of him. He knew she was gorgeous and smart, but her humor and ease at talking with his friends last night had gotten his attention. The whole time he kept thinking she was a woman he'd be happy to take home with him.

Engaging, funny, and open, she'd put his teammates at ease. More unexpected, he caught himself forgetting that they were putting on a show for his friends. There were times he believed they were in a relationship. Maybe not married, because he had no idea what having a wife was supposed to be like, but having Dana by his side felt right.

She wasn't like most women. She used her energy to bring the focus to him, instead of herself. They had actual conversations, and it wasn't all about ending the evening in bed. Although his thoughts frequently went to having sex with her, the simple truth was he enjoyed answering her silly questions and cuddling on the couch.

Soft beeps went off in the other room. He hurried into his bedroom, grabbed his watch off the dresser, and pushed the button. *Damn.*

Six o'clock, and he was due on the slope at seven. He barely had time to stretch, get suited, and meet the coach. He walked back out to the living room, glanced at Dana, and decided she'd be more comfortable in her bed.

He gingerly picked her up into his arms, along with the blanket, and carried her into the other part of the suite. An odd urge to keep her warmth pressed against him tempted him to miss practice. But the last thing he needed after narrowly missing another scandal was to miss an ordered practice. He reluctantly placed her on the bed.

She wiggled onto her side, drawing her knees up until she'd curled into a ball. He covered her with the blanket. Dana's lashes fluttered against her cheeks and she gave a contented sigh but remained sleeping. He shoved his hands in his pockets to keep from touching her.

He'd met beautiful women before—dated models and actresses all the time—but what Dana possessed exceeded all others. She was complicated, argumentative, and mysterious. Her temper rivaled his friend Dominic's girlfriend, Diana. He inhaled deeply. She called herself high maintenance, but any man would enjoy keeping her by his side and experiencing all the different sides to her.

Life would never be boring with that kind of girl. He leaned over, placed his lips on the side of her head, and inhaled. Lust hit him low. She had all the qualities that appealed to him. Even her ability to tease and get silly came in the right amount.

He'd enjoyed their talk last night. The obvious love she had for her stepbrothers came through in the stories she shared. She dedicated herself to her work at her father's company, and there were times he suspected she wanted to talk more about her job, but something held her back. Most of all, she'd forgotten about their situation last night and finally relaxed around him. He saw the real Dana for the first time.

Before he could change his mind, he walked out of the bedroom.

Fifteen minutes later, he wrote a note and left it on the dinette for Dana to find when she woke up. Then, feeling stupid, he crumbled his message and threw it toward the wastebasket. What was wrong with him?

The upcoming Olympics needed his full attention. His marriage was a fake. The more he thought of having Dana around, the less he'd concentrate on what was important. He grabbed his ski bag and left the suite.

Coach Lindhurst waited for him at the chair lift. He dropped his skis, stepped into the clip, and skied over to catch a ride to the top of the hill.

"About time," Coach said. "If your wife distracts you enough that you're late for practice, maybe you should send her home."

"Are you telling me or suggesting?" Juan turned around, caught the chair, and held up a peace sign with his two fingers as he climbed higher in the air.

Coach Lindhurst stood on the ground, shaking his head. "Don't screw up, Santiago," Coach yelled.

Juan slipped on his gloves. Despite sleeping on the couch, his shoulder suffered no ill effects. He stretched his arm over his head, breathing through the pull of the muscles. Remembering Dana's asking to help him last night instantly had him thinking about her again.

The only thing he wanted to do was get her in bed, so he could forget about the fascination he had. Hell, he'd passed fascination and was cruising in the obsessed lane. No matter what Dana did, whether she was picking up her dirty clothes or pouring a glass of water, he wanted her. Hell, even watching her walk through the suite while brushing her teeth got him hard.

Now that he was out on the mountain, he was glad he'd crumpled the note he'd written. Inviting her to ski with him after practice was through for the day was a bad idea all around. They needed to keep their lives separate. Less time around each other would make it easier to keep his hands off her. The last thing he wanted to do was screw around with her, and make it so an annulment was no longer a choice.

A divorce would send them both downhill at out of control speeds, and the end result would leave them both crippled for the rest of their lives.

The chair lift started the loop back down to the lodge. He slid off, skiing over to the others guys on the team. He'd practiced with the same men for over three years off and on. Maybe it was the competition that kept them from becoming more involved in each other's lives, or the stress of the season, but he found himself missing home.

Home was in Oregon. Soon, he'd be close enough to his real life friends to hook up with them and hang out. Life would go back to normal. Dana and the memories of their time together would be set up on the shelf, hopefully along with the gold medal he'd earn.

"You're up first, Santiago," Travis said.

"Thanks, man." He flipped his goggles down, adjusted his pole straps on his wrist, and prepared to launch.

His speed to beat: one hundred and forty miles per hour. He aimed to hit every mark today, but he wouldn't push himself to obtaining the record until he hit Germany.

The air horn blast signaled the start of the run. He pushed off. The powder descent after yesterday's snowstorm provided a smooth surface. Not a cloud in the sky, it was like skiing over the perfect ground. Juan lived for moments when the weather was clear, the trail unencumbered, and the only thing between him and the finish line was the clock.

The constant mental *tick, tick, tick,* urged him to go faster.

Straight and tight.

Stay low.

One more push, and he brought his poles in to ride out the run.

At the speed he traveled, he heard nothing but the *thrum* of his heartbeat. The rush of adrenaline that came from going faster than most people who'd put their foot to the metal on the highway gave him a rush. The risk of one fall, one mistake, knowing he defeated death doing what he loved accelerated the high.

He straightened and slowed his descent. Most people misunderstood his risky behavior on the slope, defying the rules of speed, as him being an adrenaline junky. For him, it was simple. Once he reached maximum speed, for a few seconds, it felt like he could fly.

Nothing could keep him rooted to the ground. Anything was possible. Soaring in the air meant he'd succeeded. He'd bettered his life. While proud of where he came from, his accomplishments gave his mother, his sister, and him a better life. A life without struggles.

He glanced at the clock. One hundred and twelve miles per hour. *Damn.*

"Your head's up, Juan. Put your chin down more." Coach Lindhurst tapped him on the helmet. "How are your legs?"

"Good," he muttered.

Lindhurst grabbed his polyurethane suit, stopping him from walking off. "Shoulder?"

"Fine," he said.

"Take one more run after T.T., and then you're on aerial. Coach Dobson has your gear ready," Coach Lindurst said.

A half hour later, he skied toward the clock. One hundred forty one miles per hour.

He threw his pole toward the back of the lodge to celebrate his success. His smile came quick and if he wasn't afraid of looking girly, he would've punched the air. Instead, he skied to change out of his suit. His best time this week and he was back on course.

Inside the back door of the lodge, he glanced at Dana's shop. She spotted him and waved. He lifted his chin and winked. He wanted to rush over and share the good news, but he still had one more run. One more chance to truly fly for the day.

He used the dressing room reserved for the team, and switched suits, gloves, helmet, poles, and picked out his skis. He ran his finger down the backside, testing the wax. Pumped up on positivity, he wanted to end the day with a double win.

Once he was ready, he left the room only to find Dana leaning against the wall waiting for him. He stopped.

"Hey," he said.

She smiled and stepped toward him. "Hey back. How's the skiing?"

"Good." He grinned. "Did you sleep well?"

Did she sleep well? What kind of stupid question was that?

"Yes." She shoved her hands in her jacket pockets. "I found your note."

"Yeah, well ... " He turned his head. "I know you don't have time, so I thought I'd leave you alone and let you work."

"No." She reached out and grabbed the front of his suit. "I mean, I'm glad you thought about me, and I like to ski."

"You do?"

She nodded. "Yeah."

"What time do you get off?" he asked.

He was a freight train. Full steam ahead, right into trouble. The coach was going to kill him. But right now, he could no more tell Dana he'd changed his mind than he could say no to sex if she stripped all her clothes off and stood in front of him naked.

"Any time I want. Daddy put the shop in my hands. I set my own hours, so it's no big deal if I close a little early for the day." She fought a grin. "And I'm not being a diva—I usually close early on Mondays and take Tuesdays off, because that's the slowest days of the week at the lodge."

He laughed. "Got it."

"So ... " She inhaled swiftly. "I'll meet you outside?"

He nodded. "It's a date."

She ducked her chin and walked away. He whistled, getting her attention, and waited until she turned back around.

"Come here," he said.

Her brow wrinkled, and she returned to him. "Yes?"

"Someone might be watching." He leaned closer. "You should probably kiss me, because that's what married people do."

She glanced left and right. "We're the only ones in the hallway."

"Anyone could walk in at any time," he whispered.

"That would be awkward," she whispered back.

He hovered over her upturned face. "Very."

"So, who's going to do the kissing this time?" she said, staring at his lips. "Me ... or you?"

"You," he said.

She was close enough they breathed the same air. He could practically anticipate the taste of her, and his body reacted. He hardened and held on to his poles, to keep his hands to himself.

"When should I kiss you?" she asked.

Now. Ten seconds ago. All last night. Instead, he said, "When you're ready."

She gave a slight nod. "I think I am."

"That's good," he said.

Suited up for the cold, he sweated inside his clothes. If he moved, he'd probably sway from lack of oxygen. His wife was killing him, all the while taking her own sweet time.

Dana planted her hands on his chest. "You know what, Amante Español? I think you're flirting with me."

He opened his mouth to confirm her suspicions, when she stood on her tiptoes and captured his mouth. Lightly at first, she tested him.

He held perfectly still, letting her do what she wanted. His patience paid off. Big time.

She tilted her head, and kissed him with the passion of a woman starved for one kiss. He dropped his poles and dragged her to his body, deepening the kiss.

She moaned, letting him take her weight. He sighed in pleasure. Never wanting to end the kiss, he walked her backward against the wall. He pressed his body against hers.

Thigh to thigh. Stomach to stomach. Face to face. They fit together perfectly. Her slopes fit into his contours, and he damned the suit he was wearing.

"Santiago!" Coach Dobson pulled him away from Dana.

Juan groaned. "Shit."

Chapter Eight

Dana's hands shook as she changed into her ski boots. She could blame it on Juan's kiss, but that would only be half the reason. Her fake husband had given her a real kiss. She shook her head—no, she'd given her pretend husband a kiss that left her weak. And majorly turned on.

Suddenly, she wanted to go outside and join Juan skiing more than she cared about the speed bump in her life schedule. She wanted to know more about the man who loved his family, protected her despite having no reason, ordered her to kiss him, and then sucked all the strength out of her until her ovaries begged for more.

She shoved her hands into her gloves, grabbed her skis, and walked through the door out into the snow. For a few minutes, she stood there, soaking up the activities. On this side of the lodge, the area was reserved for the Olympic team. Tourists and visitors were shuttled half a mile to the Yellow lift. Even though the team was comprised of twelve men, and not all of them would compete, they all practiced every day in hopes of filling the roster.

For every athlete, there were coaches, trainers, reporters, managers, and a whole network of people filling the area. She was surprised the lodge housed them all. She spotted T.T., and pushed her way over to him.

T.T. pointed over his shoulder. "He's on the ramp. Last run, and then you can talk to him."

"Thanks." She skied over to the fenced off area.

Not wanting to get in the way, she stayed back with the rest of the fans who'd traveled up the mountain to catch a glimpse of their favorite skier. Shielding her eyes from the glare of the sun, she peered up the mountain. Several skiers stood around, but from her distance, she couldn't tell which one was Juan.

A blast interrupted her search. She jolted, and looked at the top of the ramp. She swallowed. The long slim board, aimed down the mountain and ending on an upward pitch, seemed impossible. No one could pay her to ski down that thing.

The skier raised his arm, crouched, and the reflective marker on the top of his helmet flashed in the sunlight. Her muscles seized, and she frantically looked around at the other skiers before returning to the one on the ramp. *Juan.*

Per contract, she'd provided the needed outfits and supplies as Juan's sponsor. She'd recognize a Reese helmet anywhere. She swallowed hard.

Dana had learned to ski when she was six years old and her dad had her modeling the kids' line of winter wear. She'd attended ski bowls, tournaments, and studied durability in downhill, speed, acrobatic, aerial. But she'd never known anyone personally who flew through the air, taking a chance on their life, for what? A medal?

A louder blast from the horn elicited a scream from her before she could clamp her lips closed. Unable to move, she glued her attention on Juan. Her blood froze in her veins.

What Juan was attempting seemed impossible. When he landed—she gasped—God, if he landed, it'd kill him.

Juan reached the end of the ramp, sprang up on stiff legs laying over his skis, and soared. The crowd went silent in anticipation of the landing. Dana crouched down without taking her gaze off his flight. She wrapped her arms around her middle when he twirled. Once. Twice. And did a full turn.

"Oh shit," she whispered.

He was too close to the ground. He'd never get his feet under him. She closed her eyes. *Please let him be all right. Please let him—*

Cheers broke out all around her. She straightened, searching the end of the run for a crumpled husband.

Juan waved to the crowd and skied toward the gate. Relief left her nauseous. He was moving. He wasn't lying broken at the bottom of the hill … dead.

His smile returned when he found her at the end of the line. How dare he celebrate his jump!

"You made it," he said, sliding to a stop on the other side of the fence.

She stared, breathing hard. Her body flashed cold and hot.

He stood in front of her looking beautiful, barely out of breath, and exhilarated beyond anything she'd ever experienced herself. She wanted to slug him.

"Hey, what's wrong?" He clipped off his skis, grabbed them, and jumped the fence.

"You!" She dug the back of her ski in the snow, turned, and skied away.

Even with just his boots on, he caught her a few yards away. She slapped at his hands.

"Let me go," she said, pushing against him.

"Hold still or you're going to fall." He straddled her skis and wrapped his arms around her. "Why are you angry?"

She pursed her lips and looked away from him. Tremors came from him, and she glanced at his face. She was amusing him.

"Babe … " he said, wiping the grin off his face. "Talk to me."

"I didn't know you aerialed." She gave him one more push, but he remained holding her. "Is that how you hurt your shoulder?"

"No. I fell getting off the chair lift." He pushed her stocking hat back off her forehead.

She studied him. "You're lying," she muttered.

"Yeah." He kissed the end of her nose. "Give me five minutes to change and grab a different pair of skis and I'll race you down the hill."

"We're going slow." She staggered when he let go. "Besides, you've sucked all the fun out of spending time with you. I should leave you, and go by myself. I'm fun. What you do is plain stupid and dumb."

He ignored what she was saying and grinned as he jogged toward the lodge. She scoffed. "Men."

Second-guessing her decision to go to Germany if she had to watch him risk life and limb on the slope, she rubbed her gloved hands down the front of her coat. Why couldn't he do something safe like cross country or freestyle skiing?

Extreme sports were not her thing. Neither were men who risked everything for the thrill. She wanted dependability and security, and that wouldn't happen if her husband were dead. She rolled her eyes. She had to stop thinking of him as a permanent resident in her life.

Then she remembered the kisses. He'd promised her there'd be more. God, she hoped so. Maybe she'd grow bored with them, and then she'd remember their agreement was only for one month.

Someone grabbed her waist from behind. She screamed.

Juan laughed, snagging her hand and pulling her forward. "Come on. We only have a couple hours more of daylight. Let's hit the slope."

"I thought we had to take the shuttle." She fumbled with her pole dangling on her wrist. "I'm not allowed inside the team's area."

He let her go, and pushed ahead of her, calling over his shoulder, "You are now."

Dana hurried to keep up with him. The rules were clearly posted. She'd signed the papers and promised not to bother the Olympic team while she worked at the lodge. Her duty was to sell them supplies and convince them to wear the Reese brand. She eyed Juan.

The ski pants and gloves were definitely her father's brand, but the jacket came from Corbatt. She'd have to talk with him about making sure he was always present in Reese clothing, even when he wasn't practicing. She couldn't have her husband misrepresenting her father's company.

At the chair lift, Juan scooped her up and planted her on his lap when the chair arrived. She circled his neck with her arms to keep from falling.

"Juan." She untangled her skis from his. "What are you doing, taking me down with you when you break the other arm?"

He nuzzled her collar. "I'm spending time with you, Mrs. Santiago."

She flinched. *Mrs. Santiago?*

Juan chuckled in her ear. She whipped her gaze to his face and the warmth in his eyes caused her to melt. Then it dawned on her he wasn't calling her someone else's name, but *she* was Mrs. Santiago.

She laid her head back on his shoulder and looked ahead of them to hide her reaction. For some reason he found her humorous, and she was afraid he thought this whole charade was a joke. She knew their marriage wasn't real, but thinking he thought calling her Mrs. Santiago was something to laugh about ... well, it stung.

"Head up," he said, patting her hip.

Great. She'd never dismounted from someone's lap before, and there was a ninety-nine percent chance her skis would get tangled with his, and she'd wipe out the reigning champion before he could even reach Germany.

However, she wasn't going to tell him that and have him laugh at her again. She prepared to launch, and instead of leaving his lap, he circled his arms around her waist and jumped. She leaned forward on contact, but Juan kept her standing as they glided out of the way.

"I do know how to ski." She slipped her goggles down over her eyes. "Why don't you do your thing, and I'll do mine. I'll follow you."

His gaze dropped to the front of her coat. "That's okay. I'll follow you, and enjoy the view."

"You seriously did not just say that." She joisted her pole at his stomach. "You go first."

"Fine." He wiggled his brows, and slid past her.

She shook her head and took off after him. Going slow and enjoying the weather, she missed him veering to the left and only realized he was playing with her when he showed up beside her.

"How old are you?" she said, raising her voice.

He grinned. "Twenty-nine."

Jace was twenty-nine years old too. It was the perfect age for a man to settle down. She'd read that in *Cosmo* more than once. She'd planned for their wedding to be this year, because their ages matched the optimum survival rate for a successful marriage. She'd thought out every little step of her life, and look what that got her. Nothing.

Juan swooped in behind her, and placed his hands on her hips. She put her knees together to avoid bumping into Juan's skis.

"What are you doing now?" she said.

"Riding the rest of the trail down with you." His fingers dug into her sides and pulled her tight against him. "I don't want you to get cold."

"I'm wearing Reese clothing. I'm warmer than you are."

"I noticed." He veered them to the right and slowed their speed. "I've noticed a lot of things about you."

Her curiosity got the better of her. "Like what?" she said.

"When you don't think anyone is watching, you have a tendency to nibble on your lip as if you're thinking dirty thoughts," he said.

"Or ways to divorce you," she said.

"No." He chuckled. "I know your thoughts are sexy, because your eyelids get heavy—"

"Allergies," she replied.

"Nuh uh." He slowed them to a stop. "You know what else I noticed?"

Pleasure filled her. Jace never talked to her this way. With him it was always business. He was more apt to impress her dad so he could climb higher within the company, than excite her.

"What?" she whispered.

"Deep down, you like me, and it's killing you to admit that you want to kiss me," he said. "You enjoy having me around. I also think those naughty thoughts involve me, and I like that, babe."

Her legs shook. Not only could he say the right things, but she wanted to listen to him tell her more. She wanted his opinion about all her contradicting thoughts lately and what they meant, because she had no idea half the time. Maybe she even wanted him to convince her that the right thing to do was turn around and kiss him again. Or even talk her into sleeping with him, because since she'd met him her life had been one chaotic mess that left her wanting ... wanting ...

She squeezed her eyes closed. "We're not married."

"We're married," he said.

She shook her head. "No, what we have is a flirtationship."

"A what?" He laughed.

She shifted and moved away from him, sucking in a deep breath now that he wasn't touching her. Feeling braver, she faced him. "A flirtationship. We both enjoy flirting. We're good at flirting. That's all we can ever have."

He made that soft snorting sound he made when whatever she said entertained him, and skied ahead of her. She had no choice but to follow him.

At the lift, she let him hold her again, and she rode the chair up the side of the mountain on his lap without any refusals. To keep him off the topic of what was going on between them, she laid her head back on his shoulder and gazed up into the sky.

For the first time, she understood how he'd earned his name. Because she had a feeling Amante Español smooth-talked his way through life, and she wondered if she'd survive the month with her heart in one piece.

Chapter Nine

After dropping Dana off in the suite to take a shower after their day on the slope, Juan excused himself to take care of business. He patted his back pocket. Ever since Colton Reese paid him for taking Dana off his hands, the wedding gift he'd received had bothered the hell out of him.

Dana's accepting attitude over the check pissed him off. A woman, any woman, shouldn't spend the rest of her life questioning if a man married her for anything but love. Their temporary marriage aside, he'd never want his wife, pretend or not, to believe she wasn't first in his life.

Downstairs in the main lobby of Timber Lodge, Steve Baker, his manager for the last three years, stood in front of the desk. At his request, he'd asked Steve to fly to the lodge yesterday to meet with him.

Steve, a tall, slim, serious man who wore glasses and a blazer, held out his hand. "Juan."

"Glad you could come at such short notice." He shook.

"You pay me." Steve smiled, but quickly grew serious. "I hope you called me here because you have good news. I'd hate to see all your work turn out for nothing."

"My career is fine." Juan removed the envelope from his pocket and passed it to Steve. "There's a check in there. I need you to set up a new account. The necessary paperwork is included in the packet. I only want the money available to Dana Reese-Santiago ... her information is included too. Make sure she's the only one allowed to withdraw the money. I don't want my name anywhere on the account."

"Juan," Steve muttered. "Want to tell me what's going on?"

"No."

Steve ran his hand over his jaw. "As your manager—"

"You'll do what I ask of you," he said.

Juan refused to back down. He wanted his business kept private. One slip from anyone, and Dana would be hurt. Their marriage would be questioned, and Dana's integrity would be worth nothing.

Despite the reason for his marriage, he wouldn't allow anyone to hurt Dana. She'd stepped forward to help him and for that alone, he'd do anything to protect her.

"Okay. I'll get right on this the moment I return to the office." Steve opened his briefcase, and slipped the envelope inside. "Can you give me an idea of how much I'm carrying, in case I get stuck at the airport with people asking questions?"

"Two mill," Juan muttered. "It'd be better to wire it to an escrow before you board the plane."

Steve whistled. "She must be something."

He balled his fist. "She's my wife, and I won't have you speculating about her."

"No harm." Steve clapped him on the shoulder. "I'll see you in two weeks, and maybe I'll have the pleasure of meeting Mrs. Santiago."

Juan dipped his chin. "Later."

He watched Steve walk out the front entrance. A light snow fell outside, and Juan counted down the days until Germany. Once he finished competing this year, he needed to straighten out his life. Not only did he need to finish the business with Dana, but he was also tired of traveling, the constant pressure of being under the public's radar, answering to other people, and overthinking every move of his career.

A few weeks here, a month somewhere else, always chasing the snow. He loved skiing, and couldn't imagine hanging up his skis, but there had to be more in life than chasing the next medal. He turned away from the desk.

His unsettled feelings had only gotten stronger the last four years, but Dana's appearance in his life had him thinking about what he lacked. He loved his life. Before meeting her, he had no idea that some people used a life schedule or planned their future beyond the next four years.

His cell phone vibrated in his pocket. He pulled the phone out, smiled at the screen, and then answered. "Hola, Satchel. Let me guess … you're ready to sell me the Camaro?"

"Fuck, no." Gary, NFL linebacker for the Seattle Seahawks and one of his best friends, told Juan exactly where he could go if he even thought of touching his car.

Juan laughed. "It's nice to hear from you too."

"What's this I hear about you tying the knot?" Gary asked.

"Yeah." He kicked the heel of his sneaker against the wooden floor. "I got in a little trouble. She—Dana helped me out to get me back on the roster and it came with a marriage certificate."

"Is she for reals, man?"

"Nah." He planted his foot. "There are too many women in the world for me to settle down with one. Once the Olympics are over, we'll quietly get an annulment, and go our separate ways. No harm."

He winced at the lie. When he got married for the right reason, it'd be forever. He'd start off on the right foot, and not to a woman who he barely knew.

"Figured something was up when I read the newspaper this morning. I called Grayson, and he knew nothing about the news. Figured you'd have a reason for doing something that crazy right before competing." Gary cleared his throat. "Hey, the reason I'm calling is to see if you'll still be at the lodge on the twenty-eighth? I'm flying into Boulder, and thought I'd waste a day and see you before you leave for the games."

"Yeah, sounds good." He looked up as a woman passed him, giving him an interested look. He smiled politely as he talked with Gary. "Want me to reserve a room for you?"

"No, I fly out late the same night. On my way to a game," Gary said.

The woman sat down in the cushioned chairs in front of the window. She smiled and crooked her finger at him. He raised his brow and pointed to his chest. She nodded. He held up a finger to signal he'd be there in a few minutes.

"Okay, so give me a call the closer the day comes to remind me." Juan headed across the lounge. "I'm glad you called."

Gary roared with laughter. "Go be with your wife, Santiago."

He stopped at the reminder that he was married. "Later."

What the hell was he doing? He glanced at the woman, pivoted, and walked away.

A hand slipped behind his elbow. "Whoa there, sexy. Don't run away too fast."

The woman slid up against him. She was attractive—tall for a woman and, if he had to guess, artificially enhanced. From the hair extensions to her breasts, she yelled wealth and plastic surgeons. A typical snow bunny.

"I've heard it's customary for women to buy the first drink around here." She trailed her finger down his chest. "You look like a man who could use a bourbon on the rocks."

Her flowery scent overpowered him. He extracted his arm from her grasp, but she quickly tucked her fingers into his back pocket. Instead of amusement over her attempt to seduce him, he found her fake and pathetic.

"I wish I could, sweetheart." Juan pulled her hand out of his jeans and held it between both of his. "But I have a—"

"Wife." Dana's voice came from behind him.

He spun around and smiled. "Yes! My wife. How—" he kissed her forehead, "are you, babe? All warmed up?"

Dana refused to look at him and instead stared the other woman down. "Yes. I'm hot. So hot, honey, that I'm wondering what you're doing with—" she pointed, "her."

"Wife?" The woman backed away. "I thought you were single."

"Obviously." Dana laughed, and the response warned him he was in deep shit.

Okay, he'd noticed the woman, checked her out, but he wasn't going to do anything. He had to work his fans, keep them psyched, and motivate the youth ... although the woman was over the age of twenty-one, right? He peered closer and exhaled in relief. She was an adult.

Socializing was what he got paid to do, and harmless flirting was part of the job.

He looped his arm around Dana's shoulders and swayed her away from the front of the lodge. For his health, he ignored the other woman. He wasn't stupid. His wife was pissed.

"I thought you were staying in the room and waiting for me." He pushed the elevator button.

"You thought wrong." Dana crossed her arms.

"Babe ... " he said. "You're my wife. That woman was just another fan."

Dana's lips pursed and she shot him a death glare before going back and staring at the elevator doors. He puffed out his cheeks and exhaled slowly. Now probably wouldn't be the right time to let her know her temper amused him, and that he instantly wanted to trap all those emotions in bed and have sweat-induced sex with her.

They rode the elevator up to the third floor together. He let her stew in her anger all the way upstairs. Out in the hall, she burst ahead of him and opened their suite door first. He stepped in and shut the door.

Candles lit the table and there were two mugs sitting on the placemat. Dana rushed over and blew the candle out. His chest tightened. She'd been in the shower when he'd left.

Dana stomped to her room and shut the door. He walked to the table, picked up a mug, and brought it to his nose. He inhaled the chocolate aroma, sipped, and groaned as the bite of alcohol burned his chest. *Shit.*

He'd screwed up.

All day, he'd flirted and played on the slopes with Dana. Hell, he'd walked her back to the suite with the biggest hard-on and the desire to climb into the shower with her to warm up too, but he'd backed off. He hadn't wanted to freak her out when he was enjoying her company. Besides, if they had sex, he could kiss an annulment goodbye.

A Santiago never divorced.

He hung his head. This was all his fault.

A flirtationship. That's what she called their relationship, and she was right. He'd led her on, teased her, and left her alone in the hotel room. She'd expected more, planned for more, and he'd disappointed her. And to make her disappointment in him even worse, she'd caught another woman making the moves on him.

"Dana?" He walked to her bedroom and knocked. "Babe? Come out for a second."

Silence answered him. He turned around and leaned his back against the door. What a mess.

He couldn't tell her that he'd ran downstairs to meet his manager to make sure her future wasn't hampered by their quick, and rather stupid, decision to get married. She'd ask questions, and then he'd have to tell her what he did with the money from her dad. Regardless of what she thought of him, he wasn't going to be paid to stay married to Dana.

Call him stupid, but he wanted Dana to walk away in a month with respect for him.

Chapter Ten

Dana paced the bedroom. She slapped her forehead. *Stupid. Stupid. Stupid.*

The whole time she'd been in the shower after coming in from outside, all she could think about was Juan. How he'd teased her into enjoying their time on the slope, how they'd held hands, kissed, and touched while she pretended that what they were doing was safe. How at the end of the day, it was the best date she'd ever gone on.

A flirtationship.

Who was she fooling?

By the time she used the excuse of being cold and needing a warm shower, Juan had worked her up into a tizzy. She wanted him to keep touching her, to never stop. By the time she'd toweled off and dried her hair, she'd decided to give Juan some attention back.

He'd gone out of his way to make her day special, so she was going to repay him. Hot toddies in front of the gas fireplace, a little candlelight, and if things advanced to the bedroom, they both deserved to end their frustrations.

So, she'd planned a night of seduction. Until that bitch downstairs stole her man, and she realized she was making a fool of herself. She swept her pillow off the bed and threw it across the room. God, how stupid could she be? She was married to Amante Español. Every single woman from the age of twelve to ninety wanted a piece of him.

"Dana? Please?" Juan called through the door again.

She quietly walked toward the door and leaned against it. He sounded upset, and yet she was the one who was getting screwed over. She sat down on the floor and leaned her back against the wood.

If staying married for a month was going to make her this miserable, he deserved to suffer along with her.

"I guess if you're not going to open the door, you can listen to me then," he said. "It's true that I earned my nickname. I won't lie. There've been women in my life since I was twelve-years old. I've dated. I've had one-night stands, and left a lot of broken hearts. I'm not proud of what I've done." He paused. "Damn, this isn't coming out right. I'm trying to explain what happened tonight downstairs with that other woman."

She closed her eyes and swallowed. Each confession pierced her heart. She'd never expected him to be perfect, but the thought of him being a player disappointed her. It wasn't the fact that he had more experience to brag about than she did, but that she would never have the part of him that he shared with others. She'd always be his faux wife in their stupid pretend marriage.

She'd had an intimate relationship with Jace. Her sexual experience came from one man who scheduled sex and took a shower afterward as if it was another part of his job. She'd never lost control over her feelings before. Not the way other women did around a famous athlete ... or how she did around Juan.

"Part of my job as a member of the Olympic ski team is to appeal to the people, to build a fan base, and because of that, I've gone too far. I know I have and I'll shoulder the blame." He thumped on the door. "Babe ... even if you weren't here, and we weren't married, nothing would've happened between me and that woman downstairs. I don't have sex with women I don't know during the season. I can't afford the bad press that would come my way. The rumors and speculations are just that ... false. The troubles I get in are rarely what they appear."

"*Right*," she mouthed.

"It's true," he said. "And even if I wanted to break my own rule, I couldn't make myself be with her, because ... all I could think about was she didn't smell like you. You always smell like jasmine.

I know that's the scent, because I smelled your shampoo and read the ingredients this morning."

She covered her mouth, afraid to move. *Oh my God. He smelled my shampoo.*

"There's more about you that I like. When you let go of me after holding my hand, you always hook your finger on mine as if you don't want to lose my touch, like you're trying to hold on to the very last second. Do you know what that does to me?"

She stood and put her hand on the door handle.

"I don't know what we're doing. When we decided to get married, I thought … I thought it'd be easier than trying to talk my way back on the roster. We started out with a partnership, and today it grew into a flirtationship."

Warmth filled her, and she smiled. She was right, and he'd sensed what they had growing too.

"But you have to know I'm finding it hard to stay in the same suite as you and not touch you. I want to find out what you would do when I kiss your neck and if you'd make any noise when I sink my hands into your hair and lay you down on the bed." He cussed, and a *thunk* landed against the door. "I saw what you did out here with the drinks and the candle."

She took her hand off the handle and stepped away from the door. She'd jumped to conclusions earlier, and made a mistake. He'd already explained how he didn't have sex with women he didn't know during the season.

"So, that's it. That's what I wanted you to know. I liked what you tried to do here with the drinks, and … " He cleared your throat. "You know how I feel, but I don't know what you're thinking. I don't know what you want from me."

Her heart raced. He liked her.

He might have faked his attraction to her when they first got married, but today he'd shown her how much he enjoyed spending the day with her. She couldn't let him go to bed thinking she didn't like him too. She opened the door.

"Juan, wait," she said.

He turned around. She swallowed hard. Face to face, she hesitated. What if she'd misunderstood?

Juan held out his hand. She stepped forward and hooked his finger with hers, and his eyes softened. At that second, she knew she'd lost her heart to Juan Santiago.

Inside, she vibrated. Outside, she attempted to smile and failed. Adrenaline overpowered her ability to speak, and her thoughts misfired from one worry to one hope until she lost the capacity to think. Juan wanted her.

Her husband admitted he found her attractive, and he'd smelled her shampoo.

"Are you okay?" He hooked her neck with his free hand, pulling her close, and continued holding on to her finger.

She nodded. "I know this wasn't supposed to happen."

"It was bound to happen," he said. "I'm trying hard to be the man who promised you an annulment after I finished the games in Germany. I can't fuck it up by sleeping with you. You deserve to move on with your life, and I only want to be married once, for the right reasons. I've screwed up this time enough for both of us by making our arrangement more stressful."

She fell forward, planting her forehead against his chest. "This *is* messed up."

"I'll agree with that." He laughed softly.

Confident that she could survive the rest of her marriage without going any further with Juan, even knowing they wanted each other, she rose to her tiptoes and kissed him lightly. "Thank you."

"Let's go warm up the drinks, and sit in the living room ... far, far away from your bedroom." Juan led her into the other room.

Unsure of where they went from here, she followed. When he put a mug in her hand after heating it in the microwave, she used all her concentration on blowing across the top, cooling it to taste. When she sat on the couch, Juan sat beside her in the middle instead of on the other end.

She gulped the hot toddy and coughed. Juan lifted her cup to her lips, and she took a smaller sip as her chest and head warmed to an impossibly high degree.

"Have I told you I'm not the best cook?" She eyed the drink. "Apparently, I don't know the right measurement of alcohol either."

Juan drank, breathing through his sip. "It's fine."

She glanced at him. "Can you drink while in season?"

"It's one drink—granted, there's enough whiskey in here for four drinks—but no, drinking isn't against the rules this far out. I don't touch the stuff a week before competitions." Juan put his arm on the back of the couch behind her. "I think we both deserve to celebrate … we're married."

"Yeah, about that." She took another sip and sighed. "Sorry about earlier. I assumed the worst about you when I saw that skank hanging on you, and I know I don't have any claims a real wife would have on you."

"Don't apologize." He kissed her forehead. "If I had a real wife, I'd want her to fight for me."

She studied him. "You're not just saying that because the thought of two women rolling around on the floor in front of you jingles your balls, are you?"

"Jingles? No … " He grinned, letting that image settle. "Well, maybe a little. But I'd want my wife to make a statement. I'm hers, and she's mine."

She sipped her drink, which had cooled off enough not to burn her tongue. Juan communicated his desires more than Jace ever had. With her ex-fiancée, she'd had no idea what he was thinking most of the time they were together. Of course, she'd never pressed

76

him, because she had no aspiration to know more about him, other than the date of when they'd get married.

"Can I tell you something without you laughing?" she asked.

Juan stretched out his legs, lifted her knee, and hooked her leg over his, keeping his hand on her thigh. "Sure."

"I never loved Jace. I don't think I even liked him." She stared down into her empty cup. "My father thinks he's the greatest salesman and can do no wrong."

Juan removed her mug and set it on the floor. "Why were you going to marry him?"

She shrugged. "It was time."

"Ah, the life schedule ... "

"Yeah." She leaned her head against his shoulder. "What if I fail? It's not easy to have a social life, work, and make everything sync together for two people."

Warmed from the drink, she yawned. She didn't expect him to understand why a schedule was important to her when she didn't comprehend why she set herself up for disappointment every single time.

"You won't." Juan picked her up and situated her on his lap. "Comfortable?"

She nodded.

Facing him, one leg on each side of him, she looped her arms around his neck. It was the closest she'd ever been to him, and she looked into his incredibly dark and intense eyes.

He was going to kiss her. That much she knew. She might not know what would happen tomorrow or when they finished their deception, but he was going to kiss her, and she'd let him.

His hands went from her hips to her ass. In one tug, she was plastered against him. His heat against hers. Her tongue stuck to the roof of her mouth. Holy shit he was hot.

Scorching.

Burning.

"I need to see you," he whispered.

Juan lifted the edge of her shirt, his eyes never leaving her face. She caught her bottom lip between her teeth and let him take the material higher. She slipped her arms out of the sleeves and then her shirt was off. Juan's gaze lowered to her chest.

Pleasure flashed in his eyes. She squirmed. Hunger hit her fast and low.

"Please tell me you're going to kiss me," she whispered.

He stroked the top of her thighs. "I made you a promise when we first met. Do you remember what I said?"

She nodded. "You told me there'd be more kissing. Lots of kissing."

"Whenever and however you want." He placed his hands on her bare midriff and sucked in air. "You want a kiss? Take it, babe. It's yours to have anytime."

As if his permission meant everything in the world, she captured his lips. Soft at first, then more aggressive, she thoroughly explored his lips. Nipping, sucking, licking, tasting.

She grew dizzy, whether from the toddy or the breath Juan stole from her, she clung to him with a desperation she couldn't explain. His hand brushed her bare back. She shivered, and suddenly her bra bunched in front of her from him undoing the hook. She wiggled her arms out of the straps and dove back into the kiss.

Juan took her with him when he stretched out on the couch, tucking her along the length of him. He kissed her neck. She sank her fingers into his hair and arched her back. Heat covered her wherever his mouth landed. Her neck, her collarbone, her ribs, he paid attention to every spot except where she wanted his mouth.

"Beautiful, babe," he murmured against her breast as he took her nipple in his mouth.

She moaned from the pleasure. As if his tongue had a direct line to her core, she writhed against him. Her leg curled around his hip, seeking more.

Unable to keep her hands off him, she reached between them and cupped his hardness. His head came up and the heat from his gaze thrilled her. She wanted their clothes off, to feel his skin on hers.

"Dana … " He groaned, catching her wrist and dragging her hand up between their chests. "We need to slow down."

She shook her head. "No. It's okay."

He laid his forehead on hers. Desperate to continue, she placed her hand on his neck. His pulse beat against her palm. They were hot and heavy for each other. She'd felt the proof of how much he wanted her. Was he as frustrated as she was over their agreement not to have sex?

Before she could question him, he flipped her over him and settled her between him and the couch. Her back pressed against his front, and his legs spooned the back of hers. From this position, she couldn't read his face.

But his hardness rested between them. A reminder that they weren't finished.

"Stop overthinking what happened," he mumbled into her hair.

She raked her teeth over her lip. "I want to have sex with you," she whispered.

"I know," he said on an exhale. "If things were different, I'd be buried deep inside of you right now. I'd give anything to have your legs wrapped around me, screaming my name, but one of us has to take responsibility for what we're doing."

She moved to turn over, but his arm tightened around her, and he said, "Go to sleep, babe. Let me have this, okay?"

She refused to answer him. Stunned at the abrupt way he ended the night, she closed her eyes and willed herself not to cry. Frustrated, hurt, and unsettled, she had no idea how to take them back to a few minutes ago when she'd wanted him to make love to her.

Chapter Eleven

Juan jogged into the parking lot of Timber Lodge as daylight disappeared. Unable to face another day of hanging out with Dana in the suite after practice, he'd gone jogging after the snowplow made its final sweep down the country road. His muscles, tired from the workout earlier and his midday practice, trembled and he slowed to a walk.

The last week, living with Dana, touching her, wanting her more than he cared about the marriage paper he'd signed, he'd struggled to keep from having sex with her. She wasn't making it easy on him either.

She'd started sleeping with her bedroom door open and walking around in one of his sweatshirts in the evenings. She even slept in the damn thing. He knew that, because he'd noticed she always kicked her covers off when she slept, and when he re-covered her, the hem of the shirt bunched around her waist as if she squirmed herself to sleep.

That was how he'd found out she wore the cutest panties in all shades of wild colors and sexy styles under his oversized hoodie.

Every evening, no matter how many times he told himself they'd only cuddle and share a few kisses, they ended up doing more and more, until the only thing that remained between them was the jeans he wore.

Knowing what she wore under her clothes kept him awake each night.

He walked through the front doors of the lodge and stopped.

Dana stood with a group of six men, clipboard in hand, dressed in a pair of ski tights, fur lined jacket, and bunny boots. His chest tightened with pride. He wanted to rush over and claim his wife, but she was working. He remembered her saying she had a meeting with buyers after dinner and would be coming up to the room late.

"Our reverse cambers are top notch. I'd advise you to package them with the Telemark bindings, because they're non-releasing and provide a snug toe fit. Moderate skiers will have much less slippage. Save the release bindings for the beginners." Dana reached behind her on the desk and picked up a show model of the set. "Of course, Reese guarantees the combo for two years. You'll quickly make your money back, provided your rental history is still accurate."

A tall man to Dana's left nodded. "You've convinced me. We'll take one unit."

Dana raised her perfectly arched brows. "With the improvements made on the runs at Rainier, I'd say you're in for a boost of tourists wanting to experience the unique experience and modernization of your investment. I'd encourage you to order two units. If not now, then in the near future. Davis Enterprise sealed a partnership for apparel with Rainier last month. You'll want to take advantage of drawing in a higher clientele. And, between you and me, I sold the same package to Shasta Lodge in the spring. The results this winter have exceeded their expectations, and they're waiting on backorders."

An older man with gray hair, wearing a suit and tie, cleared his throat. "Make that three units, and we'll take a case of twin tips. The snowboarders of the past are discovering they like the mobility of free style skiing."

"Excellent." Dana wrote on the clipboard. "I'll rush the order for you, and have them to you in less than a week."

Juan stepped over and sat down, staying out of the way. Dana laughed and invited conversation while she filled out orders, and shook everyone's hands. The more Juan viewed her in her element, the more he wondered why she settled for selling clothes and equipment in the lodge, when she should be high up in her daddy's company. A natural saleswoman, she sold thousands of dollars of ski equipment every day.

He nodded at the men as they exited the lodge. Curious about the side of his wife she never showed him, he sat back and watched her clean up from her presentation. She organized the models and paperwork, and had her two suitcases packed in precisely three minutes. Then she removed her cell and put in the order personally, with the threat that if her customers didn't have the equipment in their hands within four days, she'd personally deliver them herself. He leaned back and crossed his ankles. She was a bulldog.

After Dana made sure everything was understood by the person on the other end of the phone, she said, "Throw in fifty of our new double layered helmets in a mix of sizes. Take it off my wages." She paused reaching for the suitcase. "No, do not clear that with my father. Go to HR and if they have a problem with the billing, they know where to reach me."

Surprised by her generosity, and wondering why she'd use her own money to benefit the Reese Company, Juan stood and crossed the room.

Dana slipped the phone in her pocket, hefted the bags, and turned around. Her mouth formed the cute little circle she'd often get if he surprised her, and then she caught herself and smiled.

"Hey you," she said. "How long have you been down here?"

He took her bags from her. "A few minutes. Are you wanting these downstairs or in your room?"

"Downstairs." She walked beside him. "Thanks."

Juan took the stairs. All the lights were out on the first floor underneath the lobby, because the vendors had closed shop hours ago. He waited until Dana flipped the switch and then followed her to the shop. Within minutes, he had everything put away, and she ushered him back out the door.

As they walked together to the elevator, he linked his finger with hers. "Good day?"

She shrugged. "A long day."

Once he reached their room, he pulled off his coat and removed his shirt. Dana stood beside him, watching. She blinked up at him. The naked lust in her eyes weakened him.

"I'm going to take a shower," he muttered.

He left her standing in the living room and went to his bedroom. Worn out and edgy, his body reacted to Dana instantly, a constant pleasure and torment lately. Whether she watched television, dried her hair, or poured cereal in a bowl, his body hardened. Every breath she took, he watched for her exhale. She'd perfected the simple act of putting oxygen into her body to an erotic art form.

For the last week, he'd become intimate with cold showers. They saved his life and killed him at the same time. He stepped under the spray, quickly washed, shampooed, and hopped out. Freezing his balls off couldn't stop his mind from continuing to think of what it would feel to have Dana underneath him, naked, and squeezing his body.

He hurried out to the living room, hoping to beat Dana to the couch. Maybe if he stretched out, she'd take the chair. Desperate times called for sneaky tricks. He was weak and at his lowest. He'd never be able to turn her down tonight.

The lights were out when he stepped into the front room. He frowned, looking at the fireplace. The fire was lit and the television was off. He swung his gaze across the room. *Shit.*

Dana sat curled at the end of the couch, wearing his "Ski or Go Home" sweatshirt and nothing on her legs. His lungs compressed and he fought for breath. Her bare legs were tucked underneath her, and he had a feeling she wore red panties. Because he'd already seen blue stripes, pink dots, white lace, and a slinky black thong that sent him to hyperventilating, he figured she'd wear red and kill him outright.

"Have you eaten?" he asked.

"I went to the lounge earlier and grabbed a club sandwich." She straightened. "Did you want me to order you something to eat?"

"No, I'm good." He sat in the chair, yawning. "I'm wiped."

"Hard day at practice?" She propped her elbow on the arm of the couch.

"Intense." He rolled his shoulder. "The closer we get to Germany, the more Coach pushes us. We doubled up on runs. By the time I hit the last landing, it felt like I weighed twice as much or I hit bare ground."

Dana stood and walked toward him. "I can tell you've been stressed lately."

She moved around him. He closed his eyes. She had no idea his tension came from something else … her.

Hands landed on his shoulders. He flinched and opened his eyes. "What are you doing?"

"Relax, Amante Español." She squeezed her hands, massaging his muscles. "I'm good with my hands. I'll rub the tension out of you, and then maybe you'll be able to sleep tonight."

He winched. "I sleep."

"No, you don't." She dug her thumbs into the cords of his neck. "I've heard you up at night."

She had him there. He dropped his chin to his chest. His muscles cried in joy at her manipulations. Whatever she was doing to his upper back worked. The stiffness in his shoulder eased.

Her fingers kneaded and stroked, caressing the tautness out of him. The hell with sleeping in a bed, he was going to sit right here and let her rub on him all night.

Sometime later, he realized her hands lost their strength, and Dana settled on rubbing her hands over his shoulders, down his arms, and up again. His balls tightened every time her hair brushed his bare skin. He raised his head, and came instantly alert.

When she put a kiss on his neck, he lost all control and stood. "I'm going to bed."

"What? Now?" She stood in the middle of the room, cupping her elbows in her hands.

"I have an early morning. I'll be gone by the time you get up, and after practice, I'm going out with T.T." The lies rolled off his tongue, and he backed toward the hallway. "'Night, Dana. Thanks for the backrub."

He locked himself in his bedroom and stared at the bed. Even the piece of furniture reminded him of what and who he'd left in the other room. As soon as he got the annulment, he was going to take Dana to bed for a week straight, until he worked her out of his system.

A door slammed. He lay down on his back and stared at the ceiling. Rustling came from Dana's room, and he damned himself to hell. He was an asshole.

She needed someone who would give her the attention she deserved. Instead, she was stuck with him. He wanted her worse than he wanted the gold medal, but even he had integrity. She'd only end up hating him if he slept with her. A divorce would ruin both their lives.

His disappointment in himself burned a hole in his gut. And he had no idea how to fix their problem. He couldn't send her away until after Germany and the way he wanted her, he wasn't sure he could send her away even then.

A soft click came to him. He bolted into a sitting position and cocked his head, straining to hear where the sound came from. He almost talked himself into imagining the noise when it happened again. This time from farther away.

Hurrying across the room, he threw open the door and found Dana's bedroom open. He walked over and turned on the light.

"Dana?" He walked inside her room and peered around, and then peeked in the bathroom. "Where are you?"

Not finding her, he walked out into the main part of the suite. There was a note on the table.

J—Don't worry, I'll stay away from the suite while you're here. Get your rest. D

What the fuck? He tossed the paper, and marched back to his room. His wife was not going to be out all night by herself just because he needed space.

He shoved his feet into the legs of his jeans. Anything could happen to her out there by herself. He'd find her, and bring her back.

Chapter Twelve

Dana acted without thinking out her plan. All she knew was she needed to get out of the suite before she started a huge dramatic fight with Juan. Hurt and embarrassed, she wanted to lick her wounds in private.

She understood Juan's reasoning behind keeping his distance. He wanted an annulment and to continue the no sex rule. She didn't like it, but she respected his decision. The only thing she could do was make herself scarce, and that's why she'd left the suite.

It sucked.

Call her emotional, but would sex really make that much of a difference now that they knew each other so well? She walked into the lounge, desperate to find a corner and hide out for a couple of hours until Juan was asleep for the night.

Before she could make her escape, T.T. and Joe spotted her and dragged her to the dance floor. She leaned forward. "I'm not here to party."

"What?" T.T. grabbed her hand and twirled her around to Joe.

She grabbed on to Joe's arm. "I don't want to dance."

"Sure you do." Joe kept her pinned between him and T.T.

She danced between the two of them, wondering how she was going to lie her way out of hanging with them without them knowing she'd run out on Juan.

Joe swiped a drink off the passing waiter and handed the glass to Dana with a wink. Used to his twitch, she smiled her thanks. He wasn't flirting. He had a long-term girlfriend back home.

"What's keeping Juan?" T.T. asked over the music playing.

She leaned forward. "Tired ... I came down to have a drink because I couldn't sleep."

"Bullshit." Joe patted his pocket and pulled out his cell. "He's not that much older than we are, he can handle one night out before things get serious. I'll call him and tell him to get his ass down here."

She grabbed his hand. "No. Don't."

T.T. hooked his hand around her elbow and pulled her off the dance floor. He led her to the back, down the hallway, and set her against the wall across from the bathrooms.

"What's going on?" T.T. planted both his hands on each side of her, pinning her to the wall. "Is he in trouble?"

"No … " She laughed to cover the real reason why she'd had to run from the apartment.

"I know you don't know me very well, but Juan's part of the team. I want him competing beside me. If he's doing something he shouldn't be, I need to know before Coach Lindhurst finds out." T.T. lowered his voice. "You can trust me. If he needs help, I'm there for him."

She chewed on her lip. "He's fine, really."

"Obviously something is going on, because I never got the feeling that Juan's the type of man to let his woman come down by herself when eighty percent of the people in the lounge are men." T.T. glanced down. "Why don't I walk you back up to your room?"

"No, please," she said. "God, I hate this."

T.T. frowned. "Let me help."

"You don't understand. Juan and I, we're—"

"Married." Juan spoke behind T.T.

Dana groaned. How could a girl find privacy in a hotel?

"Hey." T.T put his hand out to Juan.

Juan fisted his hand, brought back his arm, and swung through the air. Dana screamed as understanding of what Juan was going to do dawned on her. Joe came from behind them and tackled Juan, knocking him into the wall before his fist met T.T.'s face.

"Get off me." Juan pushed Joe away and scrambled to his feet.

"What the hell is going on?" T.T. grabbed Juan's shirt.

Juan pushed T.T.'s hands away and glared. "Don't touch me. Don't touch my wife."

Dana moved between them. "Stop. You're only going to get hurt, and it's the last thing either of you need."

Both men ignored her, and continued to challenge each other in a death stare. Juan hooked her waist and set her behind him. She grasped his shirt, afraid he was going to start a fight.

"Juan, please, stop. Don't get into trouble because of me. Let's go up to the room," she said.

"Want to tell me why you had my wife up against the wall in the hallway?" Juan stepped forward, chest to chest with T.T.

"Do you want to tell me why you're willing to risk your career by fighting?" T.T. shot back.

Several seconds passed. Dana held her breath. She wanted to do something to explain what had happened, but the situation was her fault to start with.

"Babe?" Juan mumbled. "Go up to the room. I'll be there after I talk to T.T."

He left her no room to argue. She scurried out from behind him and hurried down the hall. Maybe with her out of the way, the other guys could talk Juan down from whatever place he'd gone to when he found her with T.T.

Inside the suite, she paced. Uneducated on what to do when a man was about to fight over her, she picked up the hotel phone. Then she slammed the receiver back down. Who was she going to call? Laundry service?

She found her purse where she'd tossed it on the table and pulled out her cell phone. Daddy would know what to do. She pushed the button and groaned. All he'd do was inform her how she failed, and her latest disaster was all her fault.

She turned off the phone. Daddy would never believe her anyway. No man had ever fought over her.

A happy sigh escaped, surprising her. She sank down in the chair, a stupid grin on her face. Juan had followed her and actually punched T.T. to save her. Well, he'd never connected, but if Joe hadn't tackled him, Juan totally would've kicked T.T.'s ass. *Over me.*

She squee'd. For him to fight for her meant everything.

The door opened. She ran and jumped at Juan. He caught her as she wrapped her arms and legs around him. She kissed him on the cheeks, the forehead, the chin. He'd given her so many firsts in her life, and fighting for her hit the top of the list. She'd never forget this moment.

Finally, she pulled back and cupped his face in her hands. "Thank you."

He growled, and continued walking. She kissed his mouth as her body fell away. As she bounced on the mattress, Juan followed, softening his landing. Weight pressed between her legs, and she deepened the kiss.

Juan fought with his shirt, barely breaking away from her to toss the offending object to the other side of the room. Then he worked on removing her clothes, all while touching her. His hands were everywhere. His tongue and mouth touched her undressed body in delightful strokes, bites, and determination.

His arm muscles bunched and tensed. She dug her fingers in and held on. Pleasure threw her into a dizzying black hole. She only wanted him to keep going, knowing if he stopped, she'd incinerate.

Juan pulled back, breathing heavy. "I give up."

"W-what?" She gasped.

"I tried to protect us both. I didn't want a divorce ruining our lives." He placed his forehead on hers. "I thought if we kept sex out of our arrangement, an annulment would be easy for us to live with after the Olympics is over. To everyone else, we'd be viewed as never having been married … it wouldn't be valid. You'd go on to be happy, and forget about our time here. But I can't take this any longer."

She squeezed her eyes shut, unable to process that he had the strength to stop now after they were both naked. "A divorce isn't on my life schedule," she whispered.

Her eyes burned and she blinked away the moisture. Why did he have to be the responsible one out of the two of them?

"You're not listening," he said. "I can't fight how much I want you any longer. It's killing me."

"You're going to leave me? Now? Before Germany?" Her voice broke.

His mouth softened and he kissed the tip of her nose. "I'm saying, I want you more than anything, and as soon as you tell me it's okay, I'm going to make love to you all night long … and probably twice a day until we reach Germany. I know this screws up everything, but you're worth the bullshit we'll have to face when this is over."

"Seriously?" She stroked his face. "You'll ruin your life for me?"

"In a heartbeat, babe." He nodded. "If you tell me yes."

"Yes."

Faster than she could acknowledge, he'd stretched out and opened his nightstand and removed a condom. She propped herself on her elbows and got her first look at him completely naked. Her stomach fluttered in anticipation.

He was gorgeous. All hard, sculpted muscles, broad chest, and narrow hips. She sucked in a breath at the size of him.

The room tilted. Juan paused and smiled down at her.

"I bought condoms the other day, just in case. Then I spent every minute of the day talking myself out of sleeping with you." He lowered himself back between her legs and braced himself on his elbows. "No one has ever tempted me as much as you have."

Skin against skin. She was sure she'd die before they ever got around to having sex. Every cell in her body responded to the differences in their bodies. She was softer than Juan, yet they fit together perfectly. From head to toe, they were locked together.

His lips marked a trail from her mouth, down her neck, and lower, as he tasted her breasts. Sucking, licking, devouring.

She clawed at his shoulders when he sucked her to a higher level of passion. His hand wandered over her stomach, over her mound, and found the heat between her legs. She moaned and reached for more of the delightful torment he gave her.

He stroked, teased and promised, but held her back from finding release. She gyrated against his fingers, silently begging him for more. Her thighs clamped around his waist, rocking against him.

He shifted forward, and thrust into her. She gasped on a moan, pleasure shooting through her, holding her as he withdrew, plunged, and stroked her. The feelings consumed her, and she moaned his name as he sped up the rhythm of their bodies dancing.

Back and forth.

In and out.

Dip and sway.

Oh and my God.

With a cry, she shattered in the best freaking orgasm of her life, and a few heartbeats later, Juan followed her with a deep growl of his own satisfaction. Her body shuddered underneath him as pleasure rippled through her. She clung to him, afraid if she let go, he'd change his mind.

She wanted more. She wanted him every day until Germany.

Chapter Thirteen

Juan woke Dana in the most intoxicating way imaginable. She sank her hands into his hair and giggled. After making her come twice before she even opened her eyes, she was definitely awake now. He blew a raspberry on the inside of her thigh. She laughed, rolling to her side as Juan poked his head out from underneath the blanket.

His hair stuck up in all different directions. His face flushed, he grinned at her, looking mighty pleased with himself. She smiled as she trailed her finger along the strip of whiskers under his bottom lip. "Don't you have to go to practice this morning?"

He flopped onto his back, sweat covering his body. "Not until ten. Coach has a press release this morning, and the snow piled up last night. Maintenance wants to work on the ramp before we use it."

"That's good." She grew quiet.

They hadn't talked much through the night, and with daylight streaming through their window, she wondered if he'd changed his mind. Maybe he'd discovered she wasn't worth the trouble of having sex with her.

Although, that was stupid. He was right there with her, enjoying himself. But even she knew there were more important things that came into play. The Olympics.

"What are you thinking?" He rolled to face her.

"Do you regret having sex with me?"

His gaze softened and he brushed her hair back from her face. "No."

"I've been thinking … "

"When?" He raised his brows. "If you still had time to think through the night, I must not have been doing a proper job of pleasing you."

She laughed. "Don't worry. I can't even remember to breathe when you're touching me."

"Good." He kissed her. "That's the way I like it."

"Seriously, Juan. No one needs to know we've had sex. When we're done with the Olympics, we'll just tell our lawyers that we never consummated our relationship. I can tell mine that you were so busy with practice that I rarely spent any alone time with you. It'll be our secret."

"Hell," he muttered. "I can't—"

Bang. Bang. Bang.

She reached for the blanket and covered herself. "Who could that be?"

"I don't know." He rolled out of bed and grabbed his jeans off the floor. "Maybe it's one of the guys or the coach."

She groaned. "Tell them to go away."

He leaned over and kissed her again. "I'll get rid of whoever it is, and be right back."

"Hey, wait." She sat up in bed. "Did you apologize to T.T. last night?"

"We're good. He understands." He grinned and slipped out of the room.

Five minutes later Juan remained in the other room, so Dana slipped into the shower. The warm water rejuvenated her, and she hurried about her morning routine and got dressed for work. She hated opening late because there was always a crowd waiting for the shop to open.

She opened the bathroom door and almost ran into Juan. "God, you scared me to death. I thought you left the suite." She kissed him quickly, and stepped around him. "I'm going to go open the shop. There's probably a line of customers waiting for me."

"Can you hang on a few minutes?" he asked.

She glanced at him. Lines marked his forehead and he rubbed his shoulder. She approached him. "What's wrong?"

"I guess there's no easy way to break the news … "

"You're scaring me," she whispered.

"It's nothing bad. With everything going on, I forgot to mention my mom and sister were coming to visit." He grimaced. "They're here … in our suite."

"What?" She slapped her hand to her chest. "Now?"

He nodded. "It gets worse. I didn't call them and mention I'd gotten married. They heard about it from a neighbor who read about it in the newspaper, so they're … well, surprised."

"Oh, shit," she whispered. "I can't meet them. Not today or like this."

"Why not?"

She flailed her hands. "It's your family. They'll hate me."

Then it dawned on her—she had to walk out of Juan's bedroom and pretend they weren't sleeping together. "They'll know we've had sex."

The corner of his mouth twitched. "Yeah, probably."

She pushed at his chest and turned her back on him. "Go tell them I'm working, and then take them for a tour of the hotel. Buy them breakfast. Do something to get them out of the suite. I'll sneak out of here, and go hide in the shop."

Juan wrapped his arms around her from behind. "What's the real reason you don't want to meet my family?"

She sagged against him. "They're perfect. I'm not. I don't know a thing about marriage or keeping my husband happy … if this was real, I mean. They'll see right through our lies, and hate me for ruining your reputation."

He kissed the side of her head. "Be yourself. What's gone on between us isn't any of their business."

"They'll know," she said.

He turned her around, held her by the shoulders, and dipped his head to look into her eyes. "They'll see a woman who looks at me as if I'm the best thing in her life. They'll see how you're always holding my hand, and how when I go too long without talking, you always ask me what I'm thinking. If that isn't enough to convince them that I'm happy, they'll know because I'll tell them how much I adore my wife. That's not a lie. All they want from me is to know I'm happy, and you do make me happy. Okay?"

"Well, since you put it that way ... " She groaned. "I never expected you to come with a family."

"Would you not have married me?" He kissed the side of her neck.

She nudged him with her elbow. "Maybe, because I don't have any experience with a normal family ... only dysfunctional ones."

He held his hand out. "Come on. Let me introduce you to mom and Maria. Then you can go to work while I try to figure out what to do with them. I hope the hotel has an extra room available, because they're not staying with us. I don't want anything coming between you and me, because I'm going to make tonight even better than last night."

"Oh, God," she said, a thrill sweeping through her.

He laughed. "You'll be saying 'oh, God,' over and over."

She looked at him in alarm, unable to imagine anything better than what they'd already experienced. He tugged her toward the door and led her to her demise. From everything he'd told her about his family, they were perfect. He'd lost his dad when he was little, and his mom had raised him and his sister in a loving home, supporting him every step of his career.

Juan's mother clasped her hands in front of her ample breasts when they walked into the front room. When his mom's gaze swung to Dana, she made the sign of the cross before rushing toward her. A huge smile transformed her round face into a beautiful sign of acceptance.

Dana found herself captured by the five-foot tall, older woman. Dana returned her hug, smiling through her surprise at the joy on Juan's mom's face.

"I have another daughter." Juan's mother held her at arm's length and looked her over. "I'm so happy for my Juan. You must call me Ana or Mom, whichever one you'd like."

"Thank you," Dana said.

His mother held out her hand to the side. "Come, Maria, meet your new sister. Isn't she beautiful?"

Petite and beautiful with her long black hair framing her face, Maria grinned, giving Dana a quick hug. "Surprise. Knowing my brother, he gave you no warning that his family stormed the lodge."

"You're right," Dana said, making her escape to stand by Juan. "Although, I'm happy to meet you both. Juan has talked a lot about his family, and I looked forward to meeting you myself."

"We must hear all about the wedding." Ana raised her hands in the air. "After the Olympics, I want to throw a huge celebration and invite everyone we know. Did you take pictures?"

Juan laughed. "Slow down, Mom. Dana has to go to work, here at the lodge, but I'll answer all your questions over breakfast."

Dana leaned against Juan's side, at a loss of what to say. "It was very nice to meet you."

"We'll eat together. Tonight. After Dana gets done working, and can join us." Ana reached for her purse. "I'll make a list, and go shopping."

"Oh, no, please." Dana glanced between Ana and Juan. "Spend your time with Juan and catch up. I'll go shopping and cook us dinner."

"You will?" Juan asked.

His jaw twitched as if the suggestion that she cook amused him. She straightened her shoulders. Before she'd volunteered, she thought to have the meal catered in, but if Juan's mom wanted homemade food, she'd damn well cook a meal for her new family.

"I need to go if I'm going to open the shop today." She stretched and kissed Juan's cheek.

He chuckled and hooked her neck, holding her balancing on her toes. "My wife better give me a better kiss than that."

She melted, and let him kiss her. Only when Maria giggled did Juan let her go, and even that he did so reluctantly. She caught her breath and melted.

"Bye," she whispered.

"*Later,*" he mouthed.

Warmth flooded her neck, and she hurried out of the room. She jogged to the elevator, and rode down to the first floor. It wasn't until she took care of the customers waiting for her to open the Reese shop and had a moment to catch her breath that she panicked.

How was she going to impress her new mother in law and Juan's sister when she even burnt toast on a regular basis?

Chapter Fourteen

Dana wiped the counter in the kitchen and restacked the dishes she'd washed. Juan leaned against the refrigerator and studied her. He'd arrived at the suite this evening with his mom and Maria to find Dana standing in the kitchen with their dinner plates filled.

She'd served them a fabulous lasagna with a side plate of salad. But she hadn't calmed down all evening, despite the dinner going amazingly well. His mom couldn't take her eyes off his wife, who played the gracious hostess as if she'd entertained private dinners for years. But all through the meal, Dana had remained quiet and she barely touched any of her food.

Dana wrung out the dishtowel again. "Go join your family, Juan. I'll be there in a minute. I just want to clean the kitchen so we don't have a mess in the morning. Then I'll dish up dessert before your family goes back to their room."

"That can wait." He moved over, took the rag out of her hand, and turned her to face him. "What's going on? Did my family say something to upset you?"

Her gaze snapped to his eyes, and she shook her head. "God, no. They're wonderful."

"I'm glad to hear you're getting along with everyone, but you haven't relaxed at all tonight." He pulled her to him and pressed her head to his chest. "Relax. My mom's in love with you, and my sister told me she thinks you're awesome."

"Awesome?" she mumbled against his shirt.

He chuckled. "Yeah."

Her body shook, and he laughed with her, but when her body continued to tremble, he realized she wasn't finding the situation amusing, but was crying. He framed her face with his hands. "Babe? Don't cry. Talk to me."

"I'm a fake." She sniffed. "I'm not awesome, and if your mom knew who I really am and what I've done to trick you into marriage, she'd hate me. It's embarrassing, and I want to tell her the truth about how I trapped you—"

"Stop right there. It was mutual." He held her gaze. "We both jumped into getting married, so it's both our faults. We're dealing with it, right?"

"I'm not good enough for you," she whispered.

"That's not true." He caressed her cheek with his thumb.

"Oh, yeah?" She backed away and opened the oven. "Can you tell me your family will still think I'm good enough for you if they find out what I've done?"

He frowned. Either she wasn't making any sense, or he was more tired than he thought.

Dana stabbed the air, pointing inside the oven. He walked over and leaned down, peering inside.

A foil pan sat on a rack. Before he could ask what he was looking for, she reached inside. He grabbed her wrist. "Don't. You'll burn—"

But he was too late. She'd shoved her other hand inside the oven, removed the aluminum lid without using a potholder, and held the dish up. "Look."

A sticker with the words "Sally's Cuisine—We deliver" decorated the top. A bubble of hilarity tickled his throat.

Dana tossed the lid on the counter, whirled around to the fridge, and opened the freezer. "And here's dessert."

She held up a gallon of ice cream. "I didn't even have the courage to pick up some fudge to warm, because I was afraid I'd scorch the chocolate and embarrass you in front of your family. The fact is, I can't cook. I can't mix drinks. The only time I do laundry is when I run out of clothes, and lately, when that happens, I wear yours instead."

"Oh, babe … " He reached for her.

She backed away. "I'm not good enough to fit into your family, even if it's for only two more weeks."

He gazed up at the ceiling. High maintenance or not, he wasn't letting Dana feel anything but perfect for him. He picked out four bowls, four spoons, handed the silverware to Dana, and grabbed the ice cream, tucking it under his arm, while catching her free hand.

"Come on," he said.

"Juan." She dragged her feet. "Please, don't. This is embarrassing."

"No, it's normal and it's time you realized that I don't see you as anything but wonderful." He continued into the main room. "Time to dish up," he announced.

"Oh my God," Dana whispered.

Maria jumped up from the couch. "I'm stuffed, but I never turn down dessert. What kind?"

"French vanilla." Juan passed her a spoon.

Dana had a lot to learn about how a real family communicated and treated each other. He'd challenged his mom more times than he was proud of, but at the end of the day, he knew she'd have his back and he was loved. He wanted Dana to experience acceptance, even if she couldn't cook and rather keep part of herself secret to them all.

"Ah, ice cream. That brings back some good memories." His mom squeezed his arm and smiled. "Remember the summer I bought the electronic ice cream mixer?"

Juan laughed and turned to Dana, who stood back from everyone biting her lip. "When I was twelve—" he pointed at Maria "—and she was ten, Mom bought this ice cream maker at a garage sale down the street. Then she proceeded to turn Saturdays into a special family time by serving homemade ice cream to us."

Maria snorted. "Ugh. Don't remind me. Too bad we couldn't afford a therapist, because I needed one back then."

"Shush, Maria. You're being melodramatic." His mom licked her spoon and grinned at Dana. "That ice cream maker put our family on the map. In our neighborhood, Juan's achievements make the news, but I'm the famous one among our friends."

Juan scooped a heaping spoonful of ice cream in a bowl and handed it to Dana. "At the end of the summer, Mom invited the neighbors to a get-together at our house ... a backyard party. She served her famous ice cream."

He took a bite and swallowed. Dana stared at him. He waved his spoon. "Personally, I thought Mom's ice cream was the best thing I'd ever tasted. I don't know what the big deal was."

"It's gross." Maria stuck her tongue out.

"You say that now, but you ate it all summer long." His mom walked over and stood beside Dana.

"What made you famous?" Dana pulled out a chair and sat.

Juan took the seat beside her.

"It turns out that the man I bought it from used the ice cream maker as a dog food dish for his St. Bernard for years." Mom covered her mouth and laughed. "Of course, I had washed it before using it, but everyone on the block had seen the dog eat out of it on the porch. Anyway, I brought the machine out onto the picnic table, and the next thing I know, that St. Bernard knocked me down and ate up all our ice cream. There was nothing any of us could do, but stand and watch the dog eat all the ice cream."

"The dog ruined your party," Dana said.

His mom shook her head. "Oh no, not at all. I'd made extra ice cream and had twenty gallons in the freezer. I brought more out, but by that time everyone could picture the dog—with all that drool, eating out of the ice cream maker, and refused to eat any. For the next six months, we had a bowl of ice cream every night until it was gone."

"She became famous, and I was ridiculed." Maria rolled her eyes and sat at the table. "When I went to school, kids would put doggy biscuits on my desk. I never lived it down."

Juan threw back his head and laughed. "I still think it was the best ice cream."

Dana smiled. He grinned at her, glad to see her relaxing. For several minutes, they all concentrated on finishing dessert.

Finally, Dana cleared her throat. "I didn't make the lasagna."

His mom set her spoon in her bowl. Juan reached under the table and laid his hand on Dana's leg.

"To tell you the truth, I can't cook." She looked at Juan. "I wanted to impress you, so you both would think Juan had a wife who could take care of him, but I'm afraid I'm the lucky one in our marriage. Juan has a wonderful family, and he's done more for me in the short time we've been married than I can ever do in a lifetime. I'm sorry if I've disappointed you, but I thought it would be better to buy already made food and ice cream from the store, and not give you food poisoning or embarrass Juan."

Maria rose from her spot, leaned over, and hugged Dana. Juan sat back, watching his wife in awe. Never had he been so humbled and proud. Dana had given him a gift that he'd hold close to him forever. She honored his family. What Dana didn't understand was that he was the man he was today because of his mom.

"My son has been blessed his whole life. But today, he is rich." Mom held Dana's face in her hands. "He has enough money to buy anything he wants, except you. You're priceless and a gift to someone like him. Remember that, Dana. Cooking dinner … that's unimportant when I can see how he looks at you, and know he's truly happy and content, probably for the first time in his life."

Dana nodded. "Thank you."

"All right, it's getting too crowded in here." Maria picked up everyone's empty bowls. "I'm going to put these in the sink, and then Mom and I are going to our room. I'm sure Juan has an early morning. He'd probably like to relax before he goes to sleep."

Maria glanced over her shoulder on her way to the door and whispered, "Mom will fall asleep after the ten o'clock news, and I'm hitting the lounge. If you two want to join me, the drinks are on me."

Juan winked at his sister, and stayed put. Nothing would drag him away from Dana tonight. He had plans to show Dana how much he appreciated her.

Two beats after the front door closed, Dana leaned over and rested her head on his arm. "I want your family."

He kissed the top of her head. "I want you."

She raised her gaze. The same desire he was feeling reflected back in her eyes. He stood and scooped her out of the chair.

Finally, he had his wife to himself. He had an early practice scheduled for the morning, and he wasn't wasting a single minute.

Chapter Fifteen

Juan's grunt of approval this morning pleased her. Dana planted her hands on his chest. Dinner last night had turned into a wonderful evening spent with his family because of him. Afterward, she'd shown him how grateful she was of his support.

"Thank you." Dana nibbled on Juan's ear. "Again."

He'd shown her how appreciative he was of her skills in bed. Now it was her turn to show him how much having him appreciate her meant to her, and she wasn't going to let him get away with going to practice until she was through with him.

She slid down onto his erection. She caught her lip between her teeth as her body trembled in pleasure. It was always magical when they came together. He belonged in her, and she luxuriated in the contentment and excitement of having him again.

She leaned forward and braced her hands on the mattress above his shoulders. Slow, steady, and spectacular, she indulged in having him all to herself. Nobody around to distract him or calling him for an interview, just him and her, enjoying their short-term marriage.

Every nerve in her body hummed. Undulating her hips against him, she grew engrossed with how well their bodies matched. He had all the strength and power that she needed, and the understanding that she craved. Her breath left her with each of his thrusts.

Her inner muscles squeezed and caressed him with each stroke. Her head fell forward and Juan cradled her head while his hips moved and his tongue entered her mouth. Overloaded on sensations, a scream built up deep inside of her, exciting her more.

Juan gripped her hips. She arched her back and rode him hard.

"That's it, babe ... "

She let the pulsating muscles explode, and sweet release washed over her. "God, yes!"

Juan thrust one last time and shuddered underneath her. She sagged on top of him, chest to chest, and sighed as he ran his hands up and down her back. The way he touched her soul filled her with an overwhelming sense of belonging.

Once they arrived in Germany and the Olympics were over, they'd go their separate ways. Then she'd straighten out her life. She swallowed hard. Then she'd lose Juan.

"Hey." He rolled to his side, taking her with him. "You shivered. Are you cold?"

"I'm fine." She stroked his face. "Although you need to shower and hit the slopes, and I need to make a phone call to my father."

He kissed her quickly. "Five minutes, and I'll be ready."

She sat up and watched him walk into the bathroom naked. Proud and confident, he strutted and she couldn't help melting a little. She could spend every day of her life with him, and never get tired of looking at him. His body, trained for the sport of skiing, had not an ounce of extra fat.

When he hugged her, he was hard, tight, and secure. A boulder that remained steady and stable. His body matched his personality. He made her feel perfect, when she knew she had her faults.

She worried too much. She was uptight about schedules. She convinced everyone in her life that she was unemotional like her father, but Juan saw past her shields. And even though he'd witnessed her vulnerabilities, he accepted her. Even more, he respected her more for opening up to him.

He totally confused her.

Not once since they'd had sex had he brought up what would happen after they went to Germany. She'd reminded him several times that they'd better enjoy themselves while they could, because their time together was short. He always changed the subject, or took her to bed.

She sighed. His life was set on a different path than hers. He was Amante Español. She was Colton Reese's daughter.

Juan walked out of the bathroom, toweling his hair dry. He grinned. "Going in late?"

"No." She climbed out of bed. "I just wanted to kiss you goodbye for the day, before I jumped in the shower."

He tagged her waist and dragged her to his chest. His mouth came down, and she molded her body against his. He nudged her mouth open and she gasped, pushing against him.

"Juan." She covered her mouth. "You can't kiss me now."

"What?" He stalked toward her.

She backed away and ran around the bed. "You brushed your teeth. It was fine when we both had morning breath, but you can't kiss me like that before I have my turn in the bathroom."

He plopped down on the edge of the mattress, laughing. "You're cute."

"There's nothing cute about—" she stuck her tongue out, "—ugh." She hurried out of his room and into hers.

While she waited for the shower to heat, she brushed her teeth. Once she lathered her hair, she was smiling. Juan's playfulness endeared him to her.

"Babe?" Juan said.

She grabbed the towel hanging over the shower door, wiped her eyes, and peeked out. "Come here."

He stepped forward and she gave him a kiss. "Have a nice day, honey."

"Honey?" He ogled her body. "I like that."

"Me too." She splashed him with water. "Now go break records, and be careful. I don't want you worn out for later. I'm not done with you."

"I like hearing that even better." He kissed her once more. "Later."

After he left, she finished showering. She hummed while she dressed, and completed her morning ritual with ten minutes to spare.

Time to call her dad. She pushed the button on her phone while she stood in the middle of the room. From experience, she knew it was best to have lots of room to pace off her frustrations when she made her weekly call to inform him how business was going.

The call always put her in a bad mood. Nothing she did ever impressed her father. There were always other employees who sold more, worked longer hours, and would kiss her dad's ass. She wasn't an ass kisser.

Her plans went beyond Reese Enterprise and making her dad's Employee of the Month list. Some day, she'd be his sole competition, and prove to everyone that she could make it on her own without her daddy's help. In the meantime, she learned more about the business, made contacts, and waited for the right timing to put her dreams into action.

Dad's secretary answered.

"Hi, Loralei. Is my dad around?"

Of course he was. She called him every Thursday, and every Thursday he informed her she could do better with her life. She spotted one of Juan's stocking caps on the arm of the couch, and scooped it up. Maybe she'd take an early lunch, sneak outside, and watch a few minutes of Juan's practice.

She held his hat up to her nose and inhaled when her dad came on the line. "Hi, Daddy."

While her father launched into an overview of the reports she'd faxed him last night, she stretched her arm above her head and leaned to the left. Then she switched the phone to the other hand, and repeated the motion. Why was she so stiff?

She smiled to the empty room. *Juan.*

The last several days they'd taken every spare moment to have sex. She widened her stance, and stretched her hamstring. An occasional "uh huh" spoken over the phone appeased Dad and she continued to recharge her body through her yoga moves.

After five minutes, her dad ended his long list of suggestions on how she could be doing better with regards to sales and customer service. She inhaled a deep breath, prepared to agree with him, when he launched right into the Rainier account.

"Unbelievable. I taught you better than to throw money away on a sure deal." Dad exhaled loudly over the phone. "They were all set to buy, and you went ahead and threw away money by gifting a case of helmets."

"You're kidding me." She stopped moving. "You're going to tell me that spending a thousand dollars' worth of helmets to seal an almost three hundred thousand dollar order is hurting the company?"

Her only enjoyment on Thursdays came when she bested her dad. Last Thursday, it was gaining the Shasta account. Today, she'd outsmarted him. Because victory was sweet, she let him lecture her until he thought he'd proven his point.

Then she dropped the shocker.

"Look on the invoice, and you'll see that I used my own account to send the helmets. Besides the commission I made on the Rainier sales, I'm happy to report that yesterday I received an order from Bockman, triple the size of the Rainier order. Let me refresh your memory, Dad." She paused to get his attention. "Reese has never been able to get a spot on the Bockman list of buyers in over twenty years."

Her father's silence boosted her confidence. She danced a few steps and plopped down on the couch, no longer needing to pace.

"So, besides the three hundred grand, I brought in almost a million from a new account, an account you drool over in your sleep, and all it cost you is the embarrassment of knowing your daughter used a grand of her own money. Money you know the commission will cover times twenty." She crossed her legs and swung her foot. "Feel free to write me an early Christmas bonus, because I do believe I climbed the ladder right over all your wannabes, and I'm sitting in the Saleswoman of the Year seat."

A formal grunt of acceptance from her dad, and Dana changed the subject to one that made the dreaded Thursday phone call worth every minute of pain. "How are the boys?"

"Max and Alex miss you. Jonathon has a new girlfriend—" he said something to his secretary, "—she's from the Randolf family. The whole situation is causing undue stress to my wife, so I'm taking her to the Bahamas next month."

She sat up straighter. "Where are the boys staying?"

"They're in school, so—"

"I'll come over and stay at the house." She scratched the palm of her hand with her fingernail. "That way they won't miss school, and I can work from your office. I'm closing the shop here a week early, because I'm going with Juan to Germany. I'll be back in time to take care of them."

Her dad asked about Juan, and she covered with her pre-planned excuse. "You know he'll be busy with all the interviews, sponsored events, and traveling around giving live interviews. It'll be the perfect time for me to stay with the boys while he's busy."

Excited that she'd have a distraction for when she'd be dealing with having Juan gone from her life, she ended the call. She jumped to her feet, and shimmied around the room. "Yes. Yes. Yes."

"Good news?" Juan said.

She screamed and whirled around. "I thought you were gone."

"I came back for my hat." He pointed to his stocking cap on the couch.

She sagged in relief, her hand pressed to her chest. "You should learn to make noise when you come in the suite. I think I'm having a heart attack."

He chuckled. "Your dad's phone call make you happy?"

She waved her hand. "Regardless that I made him money and gained him more business, I've still disappointed him because I refuse to follow his example. Same ol' thing, but I have good news."

"What?"

"I get to take care of my brothers for a week next month while their mom and our dad go out of town." She handed him his hat.

He sat down beside her on the couch. "I can see that makes you happy."

Silence stretched between them. She inhaled deeply, her heartbeat slowing down after Juan scared her.

"I'll walk down with you. It's time to open the shop," she said.

"Hang on a minute." Juan ran his hands over his face. "Why do you let your father de-value what you put into his company? I've watched how much you do, and though you're only in charge of one shop, you're working in sales and distributing large orders outside the regular venue. Yet from the sound of it, your dad doesn't give you the accolades you deserve. Why?"

"It doesn't matter." She moved to stand, but he stopped her. "Honestly, I could discover a new country, and he'd still find fault in how I accomplished to make history."

"You deserve the acknowledgement for all the work you do," he said quietly.

The room pressed in on her. She forced a swallow over the pressure in her chest. She'd learned a long time ago there was no pleasing her father when it came to business. His drive to success outweighed anything his children could do. For Dad, business came first and family second or third, she wasn't sure, because he enjoyed playing golf and would often miss birthdays and holidays because he had an eighteen hole to shoot.

"Maybe." She glanced at Juan. "But I'm okay with what I do. I'm proud of myself. I don't need someone else patting me on the head and telling me I did a good job."

"Are you content to continue working at Reese? You're not just selling ski equipment; you're running the whole damn company from a hotel room. I imagine your dad has other salesmen or women, using up company expenses traveling to every ski resort and lodge in the world doing what you're doing here." He linked his finger through hers. "What's your dream?"

She shook her head. "No dreams. I have a life schedule. Working for Daddy is just a way to finance my life. If you want to know what I'll be doing in five, ten, twenty years, I can tell you."

She hoped he wouldn't ask. Right now, her life schedule was off course.

"Tell me what you're going to be doing in five years," he said.

Dammit. She looked away, and debated whether to lie or shrug off his question. He squeezed his finger, tightening their bond.

So she told him the truth.

"In five years, I'll be married and trying to get pregnant with my first child. My husband will be so in love with me, he'll work from home because he can't stand to be away from me. Together, we'll spend our days traveling, visiting ski resorts, and selling ski equipment that exceeds the durability of any competitors around, including the Reese company." She blinked back the tears blurring her vision.

"Do you have a product?" Juan kissed the tip of her nose.

She nodded. "Prototypes. No one has seen them. I'm biding my time. I refuse to show my dad. He doesn't have a clue I want to give him a run for his money in the same market he made a name for himself in."

"What's stopping you from going out on your own now?"

She rolled her eyes. "It's not time ... my life—"

"Ah, your schedule." He kissed her again. "Go to work, babe. I need to go practice."

The rest of the day she tried to shake of her melancholy attitude, but she kept going back to what Juan said after she told him about her life schedule. He didn't ask her who she'd be married to or laugh about her dream of a love that lasts forever. He didn't acknowledge that their marriage was a farce, and she'd planned to quickly forget about her time spent with him.

It was time to face the fact that Juan wasn't going to be the man loving her in five years. The thought hurt her heart.

Chapter Sixteen

Two days before the flight to Germany, Juan eased out of the hot tub determined to make the most of his time with Dana. He'd put in a full day of skiing on top of having a physical, going through the lab work to verify he still qualified to compete, and having the physical therapist look at his shoulder.

Dana was out shopping for the trip, and he wished she were here now. He threw the towel around his neck and let the cold air lower his body temperature. It'd do no good to go inside and fall asleep when he'd looked forward to spending tonight with his wife.

He walked inside and quickly showered. As he stepped out, Dana rushed into the bathroom.

"Oh, good." She smiled, fairly bouncing in excitement. "You need to hurry and get dressed."

"Why?" He shook out his hair, ran his fingers through, and swept it off his forehead.

"Because I have the biggest surprise for you. Like the coolest thing ever happened to me when I was downstairs." Her eyes grew round. "You will not believe who I met today."

His breath hitched and the first thought that entered his head was that she'd discovered someone else who would slide into her life schedule and kick him out. He turned around and put on his deodorant. He had no desire to walk out of the room.

"Must be someone special to get you this excited." Hell, he was even jealous of whoever put the smile on her face today. It wasn't him. He'd been busy, and regretted the time away from her.

"He is!" She bit down on her lip and rocked forward on her feet. "He's going to blow you away.

He growled. *He. So it is a man. Shit.*

"Hurry." She stepped over and threw her arms around his waist. "We don't want to keep him waiting."

In the mirror, he took in her flushed cheeks, her excitement, her energy. He wanted to be the one to thrill her beyond words. He hadn't said anything, because it wasn't his place to discourage her, she had enough people holding her back, but he'd like to take her damn life schedule and throw it out the fucking window.

He was her husband. What happened to her getting excited over seeing him? Hell, he was standing here without any clothes on, and she'd barely noticed him.

"Please." She pulled on his arm. "You look gorgeous."

About time she paid attention. He hooked her neck, pulling her closer, and kissed her.

She planted her hands on his stomach and pressed into him, kissing him back. With her focus on him again, he calmed. He pulled back and gazed down at her. "Missed you, babe."

"I missed you too," she said. "Now hurry, get dressed."

"Okay, okay." He walked out to the bedroom, pulled on a pair of jeans and sweatshirt, and sat down to put on his socks and shoes. "This better not be a joke and Maria talked you into dragging me out of the room only to have her and Mom here for the evening. We had plans ... alone."

"Of course not. Your mom and Maria are already on their way to Germany. They left an hour ago, didn't they say goodbye to you?" She frowned.

He shook his head. "I was busy ... "

"Oh, well we'll catch up with them when we arrive for the Games." She bounced back into her excitement. "This surprise is ... well, you'll have to see. It's huge."

Dana led him into the living room. He held her hips, not wanting her far away from him. He'd gone all day without her, and wanted her more than he needed to see her big surprise.

In the living room, Gary Satchel lounged on the couch. Juan grinned and lifted his chin at his good friend. Damn. He'd forgotten all about Gary coming to visit.

"Juan—" Dana turned and beamed at him before swinging both arms toward the couch "—meet Gary Satchal, only the best NFL football player ever. He also plays on my favorite team, the Seattle Seahawks."

Gary pushed all six-foot-four inches and two-hundred-and-fifty pounds off the couch and stood. The smile on Gary's face was a reflection on how much amusement he was getting from Dana's obvious fangirl moment. Juan would've decked him if he weren't so happy to see his friend himself.

Juan stepped forward and held out his hand. "Gary Fatchel?"

"Satchel." Gary shook Juan's hand, squeezing harder than normal. "You're that guy … um … John … "

"Juan." He held his laughter inside.

"Oh my God." Dana wrapped her arms around Juan's waist. "I was downstairs and I spotted him right away. How could I not? Even without the Seahawk sweatshirt, I would've known him anywhere. He's a ton of muscle. So, I told him all about you, seeing how you're both athletes, and begged him to come to our suite and meet you in person. Isn't this great?"

"I guess." Juan shrugged. "Not much of a football fan, babe."

Gary cleared his throat. "And … uh … I've never skied."

"Seriously?" Dana shook her head. "What planet do you both live on?"

"Relax." Juan moved around Dana. "You sit and talk with Fatch—"

"Satchel," she said.

"Right. Satchel … the football player from Pittsburgh—"

"Seattle." Dana groaned. "Really, Juan. He was recently traded to the Cowboys. I can't believe you're not a football fan."

"Don't need to be, babe. I'm a skier." He kissed her. "Go ahead and act all silly and have your moment. I'll grab him a beer, 'kay?"

Dana broke out in a smile and nodded. "Thanks."

Juan waited until Dana turned her back to him, and flipped Gary the middle finger. Son of a bitch was enjoying every moment of his wife fawning over him. Gary raised his brows and all but ignored him.

Juan walked into the kitchen and retrieved a beer. It was too close to competition for him to drink, but he sure could use one to get him through the evening. First chance he got, he'd slap Gary on the back for stopping by, tell him he'd catch up later, and then show him the door.

Best friend or not, he wanted nothing to come between him and his wife. He was running out of time with her.

He returned to the room, passed Gary a beer, and because his wife sat beside Gary—who took up half the couch—Juan resigned himself to the chair across from them.

Dana handed Gary a pen and paper, and mentioned her stepbrothers' names. Juan stretched out his legs and clasped his hands behind his head. He learned something new about his wife every day. He had no idea she was a football fan. Maybe he should mention that he had a connection and could take her to a few of the Seahawk games once he was finished with the Olympics.

"Thank you so much." Dana set the paper on the coffee table. "The boys are going to freak. Oh! Can I get a picture too?"

Dana dug her phone out of her pocket, stood, and passed it to Juan, and plopped back down on the couch, practically sitting in Gary's lap. He growled, took the picture, and relaxed when Dana scooted a few inches away from Gary.

An uncomfortable silence filled the room. Juan enjoyed every minute of it.

"So, Fa-Satchel, tell me. Does being a big football star get you many women?" Juan resumed his bored sitting position.

"Juan!" Dana threw him a death stare.

"What?" He looked at Gary. "It's an honest question. You came with my wife to our room, and I wonder why. Do you normally have women stroking your … ego wherever you go?"

Gary laid his arm behind Dana on the couch. "Actually. Yes. I do."

Dana blushed and continued to stare bug-eyed at Juan, willing him to stop. He couldn't help himself. This was the most fun he'd had all day.

"Was that your plan with Dana?" Juan sat forward, bracing his elbows on his knees.

Gary looked between Dana and him, read the situation right, and stood. "Still is my plan. She's a sexy woman, and I have free time before I fly out for the game. I don't see her hanging off you, so—" Gary patted his chest, "—she's fair game for a man like me."

Juan flew out of the chair and dove across the coffee table. Dana screamed and, thank God, Gary caught him and they tumbled to the couch. He faked a punch to Gary's stomach, and then exaggerated the painful cry when he received a punch to his back.

"Stop it!" Dana pulled on Gary's arm. "Don't hurt his shoulder."

He buried his face in Gary's back, laughing his head off while holding Gary in a headlock as he was tossed and rolled onto the floor. A pillow smacked him in the head.

"You can't fight. You'll get kicked off the team." She kicked out, and Gary grunted.

Juan couldn't go on. He let go of Gary and collapsed onto his back on the floor. He could barely keep his eyes open, he was laughing so hard.

"She's something else, bro." Gary heaved himself off the floor and stuck his hand out.

Juan grasped his wrist, and sprang to his feet. "Gary, meet my wife, Dana … the avenging angel, powerful enough to kick a linebacker's ass."

"What?" Dana's jaw dropped opened. "Are you kidding me? You know him … like know, know him?"

Juan stepped over and looped his arm around Dana's shoulders, drawing her to his side. "Gary's one of my best friends, babe. I've known him forever … along with Crista, Bruce, Grayson, and Dominic. Remember, I told you who my friends were."

"Dude. You never said it was Gary freaking Satchel." She hurled the pillow at his head. "I can't believe you let me go on and make a fool of myself."

Gary tossed his head back. "I'm going to have that name put on my jersey. Gary Freaking Satchel. I love it."

Dana glared at her idol. "I hate you."

Not intimidated in the least, Gary strolled right over, picked Dana up in one of his famous bear hugs, and smacked a huge kiss to her cheek. "Congratulations on your marriage. You've captured one of the best men I know."

She rolled her eyes. "I hate him right now too."

Gary laughed and set her back on her feet. Juan moved in and nuzzled her neck. "Sorry, I couldn't help it. You were too excited over seeing another man. I had to prove I was worth being married to by protecting my woman."

She snorted, but found his hand. Together they walked over to the couch. He planned to catch up on all the news back home with Gary and send him on his way. This could be the last chance he had with his wife, and then he'd focus on winning the gold.

Chapter Seventeen

The tender, perfect touch of Juan's lips caressed her breast. Dana arched against him as he moved back and forth between her mouth, her neck, and her breasts, eliciting a thrill through her.

He settled his hand on her stomach. The warmth penetrated clear through her body and she squirmed underneath him. He kissed the sensitive spot at the base of her neck, blew on the area, and she quivered. She wanted him to touch her where she needed him most, but he never moved his hand.

His tongue swept inside her mouth. She moaned. And finally his hand trailed further down, burning a path from her stomach to between her legs. Every nerve jumped and settled in her core as his hand found her sex.

The intimacy aroused her. She clasped his hair in her fist, holding herself back. She floated on her arousal. The warm, wet, heat from mouth followed his hand. She gasped for breath as he situated himself between her thighs.

Electricity shot through her as he found her sweet spot. Her hips shot off the bed, while her legs fell open. Pleasure built inside of her, and she grabbed onto the bedspread, urging him for more.

He added his finger, moving slowly, filling her, without taking his mouth off her. The tension of leaving today faded to something unbelievably delicious, and she lost track of time.

She stretched, pulled, and moved against him, caught up in what he was doing to her. Yet, in the back of her mind, she knew it would be their last time together in bed, having sex. The moment was bittersweet, but she promised herself she'd be strong for Juan.

He'd gone back on his theory of having no sex a week before a competition, and changed it to no sex in Germany in the hopes that it'd make him more aware, stronger, and boost his endurance.

She warmed, knowing she had the power to relax him to the point where he needed her more than she needed him.

Deep down, she wanted to believe she meant more to him than his saving grace to stay on the team. They'd become friends. They'd taken their flirtationship all the way to the top, and she knew that once she walked away, her life would never be the same again.

Juan crawled up her body and hovered above her. He gazed into her eyes. "I lost you for a moment."

She cocked her head to the side, and stroked his face. "I'm here."

"What are you thinking?"

His heart beat against her chest. For him, she'd do what must be done. "Imagining you winning the gold."

He frowned. "Babe ... "

"Do it for me, honey. Give me right now and tonight. Then put your heart and soul into winning. Make everything we've gone through together mean something. Let me have the memories of being with the man everyone will talk about for years." She inhaled deeply, and forced a grin. "I want you on the side of a Wheaties box."

He smiled tenderly and kissed the tip of her nose. She swallowed hard. God, she was going to miss the nose kissing.

"Let's both win the gold." He slipped inside of her. "Together."

The intense buildup of pressure filling her was her undoing. Her chest heaved in a sob, and she used the emotion to give everything to Juan. In sync, souls touching, she never took her gaze off him. The moment was so powerful it rocked her right off her life schedule, and she reached out and grasped what he offered.

Greedily, she held him, moved him, stroked him. She'd remember every second and play it back in her head for the rest of her life. Although she'd tried to deny her attraction, her flirting, her lies that she was faking their relationship, she'd somehow fallen in love with her husband.

"That's it, babe." Juan plunged deeper, harder, taking her higher. "Come for me."

Her muscles constricted and as if to hold him inside of her forever, she screamed out his name, bucking against him as he held her. He shuddered in her arms, and laid his head against her neck. Locked together, legs entwined, arms holding one another, they breathed in rhythm of their hearts.

Long after she'd gathered air into her lungs, and Juan's heartbeat slowed until she could no longer separate it from her own, she lay there silently, afraid to cry for the finalization of the act. For if she cried, she was afraid she'd never be able to stop.

"Dana," he whispered. "We'll be okay."

She nodded, and whispered back. "I know."

Juan rolled off her, and this time he kept moving and got out of bed. She shivered, missing his warmth, his body, him.

"I'm going to hop in the shower and then I need to go out. Photographers are here, and they want team photos before we leave for the airport." He paused at the bathroom door. "I'll send someone up to carry our luggage when it's time to head out. Do you need me to do anything for you before I'm pulled away with team stuff?"

She shook her head. "No, I think I'm all set. I shipped most of my things yesterday to my dad's house, and only kept two pieces of luggage for our trip. Someone from Reese is coming to close the shop tomorrow, so if I run into anything I forgot to send on, I'll go ahead and let them take it back for me."

"Okay." His gaze softened before he walked into the bathroom.

Dana reluctantly left the bed and walked to her own room. Each step took her away from Juan. No longer excited about going to Germany and seeing Ana and Maria, or cheering on Juan, she wanted to crawl under the covers and have a good cry.

But, because she was a Reese and she could use the opportunity to open doors with more distributors once they arrived at Germany, she went through the motions of taking a shower, getting dressed, and saying goodbye to married life. She'd pretend to be strong, because the last thing she wanted to do was worry Juan when the gold was on the line.

When the crew of men came to carry Juan's equipment and his luggage down to the awaiting cars, she followed them downstairs. All business and no emotions, she concentrated on going through the steps to getting her life back.

Cheers went up outside the lodge. She pushed through the doors, and took in the crowd. At least two hundred people lined the edges of the two-lane street leading away from the lodge. American flags waved from their hands. Signs fluttered in the wind, and she smiled, noticing that most of them had Juan's name or Amante Español printed in big, bold, red letters. She searched for the team, and found them standing beside three limousines.

A sea of red, white, and blue, they all looked serious and professional. Juan stood with his hands clasped behind his back. He looked at the cameras without smiling, lost in his own world. Even without the outward show of happiness, the excitement rolled off him. He rocked from his heels to his toes. His jaw twitched, and she wanted to rush up to him and caress her hand down the side of his face and watch him soften under her touch.

As the scene in front of her blurred, she realized she was crying. She'd never been more proud of anyone in her life the way she was of Juan and what he'd already accomplished. It wouldn't take a gold medal to impress her. He was already a winner to her.

Juan raised his hand in her direction, spoke to T.T., and slipped away from the group. He jogged over to her. She dashed her hand over her cheeks and smiled, while inside she crumbled.

"Hey." He hooked her waist and pulled her closer. "I've got a car to take you to the airport. I'm sorry we can't ride together, but the team has to go with the security team. Once we get to the airport, go ahead and board. I moved you up to first class and that way you can sit beside me on the flight."

"Sure, that's fine." She patted his stomach. "Are you having fun and enjoying your big departure?"

"Yeah." He walked with her to the cars. "Pretty big crowd. This is when everything seems to hit me that it's time, it's real."

She waved to T.T. and Joe. "It is real. Three more days and you'll be competing in your first event."

She was babbling. He knew his schedule and had a whole montage of people to remind him if he forgot. He needed to concentrate on doing his job, and not catering to her to make sure she had a ride to the airport or her luggage made it on the plane.

Even when his life became too busy, he never failed to focus on her and make sure she handled everything okay. His attention, when she was around, centered on her, and she loved that about him. In the last month, she'd blossomed.

The biggest thing she could do to support him was let him go. He'd made it to the end, and stayed out of trouble. He wouldn't screw anything up this close to the Olympics. He no longer needed her, or their marriage.

She stopped and turned. "I have something I need to tell you."

"Okay." He brushed her hair behind her shoulder.

The last few days, she knew their time would come down to this moment. She'd argued with herself, changed her mind a million times, and came up with every excuse why she had to stay with him in Germany, and each time that little voice in her head told her she'd completed her end of the bargain. Their time was over. They'd successfully stayed married and saved Juan's career. He was going to the Olympics.

Juan no longer needed her.

He'd settle down, and dedicate himself to training. His head was in a good place to compete. She stared up into his dark eyes.

He'd never admitted that his feelings toward her were real past enjoying her in bed. Or that their relationship was anything more than a fake marriage with benefits.

What he had told her over and over was he wanted her, sexually. She amused him more than anything when they were out of bed. He also enjoyed her company and they had similar tastes. Those were all things he freely confessed, but he'd never once admitted to falling in love with her. He'd never once spoken of what would happen after the Olympics were over. He never once asked her to make their marriage real.

"I'm not going to Germany." She bit her lip, and when he didn't say anything, she continued. "We stayed married for a month and so far, Amante Español, you've turned into a prime example of a professional athlete."

"Babe ... "

She grasped his hand. "You need to concentrate on the games. You'll be so busy, I'll be bored most of the time shut in the hotel room. After the Olympics your life will be thrust into total chaos. You'll have interviews and television shows to appear on. Besides, without me there, you can use my seat to hold all your medals when you come back to the states."

Juan gazed off into the distance. "I'm not ready to let you go," he whispered.

"I know." She squeezed his hand. "But it's time. It'll be easier this way. You need to concentrate on you. This is important."

He looked at her. His jaw ticked, and the intense way he studied her hurt. Her chest tightened painfully, and her knees shook.

"You have to go with me," he said.

Hope rose inside of her. She leaned toward him.

"It only makes sense. You represent the Reese Company, my sponsor. It's a perfect excuse to show your father how much work you do behind the scenes and have him acknowledge you. Think of all the contacts and people who will view the Reese line and want to put in orders." He opened the car door. "I'll meet you at the airport. Make sure you're there. Okay?"

"But—"

His mouth hardened. "You're going with me."

She climbed into the car. Juan gave her one more look, letting her know he wasn't messing around and she had better be on the plane when he arrived. She clamped her mouth shut. She had to keep moving forward, despite him trying to make their situation harder on her.

The door shut. She stared out the darkened window. Juan remained standing beside the car. She'd hoped for something from him that she could latch on to and hold to her heart. But he'd talked business, not love.

"To the airport, Ms.?" The driver peered at her in the rearview mirror.

She cleared her throat. "Yes, thank you."

Juan was right. Her dad expected her to bring Reese to the top with their exposure at the Olympics. Behind the marriage gift her dad had given Juan, and his sponsorship while he competed, was a shrewd businessman. He wasn't handing out money to make her happy. Colton Reese did what he did best. He'd bought her a husband and a way to make money for his company.

She stared out the windows. How could she forget that Juan walked away from their marriage two million dollars richer, just for taking her off her daddy's hands?

She dropped her gaze to her hands on her lap. Her left ring finger lay bare. She'd given Juan the ring meant for Jace, but she walked away with nothing. Now Juan would come out of the faux marriage richer, and she would go home with a broken heart.

Chapter Eighteen

Two days in Germany, and Dana hadn't had a moment to think about anything but business. She closed her laptop and handed the computer to Barbara, who worked the desk at the hotel.

"Thank you." She waited while they secured her laptop in the safe.

To her surprise, Juan had introduced her to the skiers from other countries, and they'd pushed her toward the managers representing each team. Before she knew what was happening, she had to set up times to meet each one individually, and they were more than willing to listen to her spiel about the benefits of using Reese products.

She wasn't sure how she'd handle the presentations at first, but after obtaining permission to borrow the hotel's fax machine and hooking to Wi-Fi, she'd used her laptop to gain entrance to the Reese website. Along with having Juan present to show off his gear and skis while he practiced on the slopes, she'd been able to show potential clients the Reese products online, and the end result was that she'd sold more orders than she had in the last six months, which was saying a lot. She'd already outsold every employee working at Reese this year.

Her father's giddiness as the orders rolled in swept her into a good mood. Overseas orders were rare, but not anymore. By this time next year, they'd quadruple their clientele.

She only wished she had her plans and models for the ski equipment she was designing on her own. The exposure would've launched her career, and she could finally break away from the family business. Determined to hit the next winter Olympics with her own line, she shoved her life schedule to the back of her mind.

She had to jump at the opportunity presented to her, and it was time to take the leap on her own.

"Dana!" Maria waved and hurried toward her, dragging another woman with her.

"Hello ... there you are. I was wondering what you and your mom were doing today." She kissed Maria's cheek.

"She's resting, and I'm having the time of my life." Maria backed away, pointing at the other woman. "This is Crista. She's one of Juan's friends. Do me a favor and keep her company until Bruce shows up ... I have to leave."

Dana stepped forward. "Where are you going?"

"Denmark." Maria giggled, waving over her shoulder.

"What? Are you crazy? Your brother is going to ski. You can't leave the hotel, much less the country." Dana gawked at Maria.

"She's wild, but not crazy. She only meant she was going to hang out with the guys from the Denmark ski team." Crista stepped over beside her. "Have you seen those boys?"

"No." Dana exhaled in relief and smiled at Crista. "You're exactly like I pictured you."

Crista's eyes sparkled and she pushed the hood on her jacket back, letting her blonde hair tumble over her shoulders. Slim and in perfect shape, Crista was the picture of strength and confidence. Dana leaned closer. "Although to be honest, I hated you when I first heard your name."

"Why?" Crista asked. "What did I do?"

"After I married Juan, I overheard him on the phone with you, and I thought you were his girlfriend." She shook her head when Crista laughed. "You two are close, and I was jealous."

Crista pointed toward the ceiling. Dana's gaze followed her finger to the giant banner with Juan's picture on it. "Juan's ego is as big as his head is in that picture. It goes with the territory. All athletes have fans ready to stroke their self-confidence, but my friends—and that includes Grayson, Dominic, Bruce, Gary, and Juan—are just little boys to me who need a lot of attention and guidance, or they'd screw up every relationship they have. I'm their go-to girl for advice. Plus, when we're together, we can be real with each other when everyone else wants to lie to us. I'm the same way with them. Sometimes it's hard for their girlfriends or wives to understand our relationship … but you will. You'll see." Crista leaned closer and lowered her voice. "Just don't hurt him, or I'll come after you with my claws and scratch your eyes out."

"Gotcha," Dana mumbled.

Crista jumped and waved her arm over her head. "There's Bruce."

Dana clasped her hands in front of her, totally out of her element. She knew these people from stories Juan had shared with her. Crista was the Ironman champion; Bruce was a world-class bass fisherman. She stood back as Crista flew into Bruce's arms.

"You're here." Crista squeezed his neck.

He pretended to struggle for breath. "We'd planned our trip for two months, sweetheart. I don't know why you're acting surprised to see me."

"Because I haven't seen your ugly face for three months, idiot," Crista said with a smile. "I can't believe you missed the flight, but I'm glad you made it. It wouldn't be the same without you here."

Rugged and sexy, with sun-streaked blond hair, Bruce slapped Crista's butt and laughed when she punched him in the shoulder. Dana smiled, relaxing. Apparently Crista was just one of the guys around Juan.

"Bruce, meet Juan's wife Dana." Crista pushed Bruce forward.

Bruce's brows rose and he rocked back on the heels of his boots. "Bullshit."

"W-what?" Dana's heart raced.

"You can't be married to Amante Español. You're way too beautiful to saddle yourself with him." He slowly approached her and wrapped her in a tender hug. "Run away with me. We'll go to

Acapulco. No more sweaters and cold weather where I'll be taking you. Only you, me, bikinis, and margaritas as far as you can see."

She stared over Bruce's shoulder at Crista and mouthed, "Is he serious?"

Crista shook her head and rolled her eyes.

Once Bruce let her go, she said. "Sorry. I get sea sick, and Juan's a little possessive. He fought Gary for me, and won."

Bruce laughed, and because his eyes crinkled in the corner and the most pleasing deep sound came out of his mouth, she couldn't help but join him. He kissed her cheek. "Now I know you're lying. No one can beat up Gary—well, maybe Dominic could give him a run for his money—but we little guys would get our ass kicked."

"Enough talking." Crista wormed her way between Dana and Bruce. "We've got a half hour to make our way to the fence line."

"Oh, you better go." Dana nodded and grabbed her bag. "I've got a ticket in the seats with Juan's mom and sister, so I better put my stuff in my room first."

Crista pulled out three tickets from her pocket. "Not anymore. Surprise."

Dana grabbed her wrist. "How did you get those? Nobody but the press and the entourage can get down there."

"Juan. He sent them to me with detailed instructions that Bruce and I could only use them if we made sure you made it down to the front with us." Crista grinned. "I'm sure he already gave Ana and Maria their passes."

Dana's stomach knotted. Being accepted by his friends, loved by his family, and treated special by Juan left her with mixed emotions. She wanted to believe things would continue, but they wouldn't. And she hated herself for fooling everyone. They'd hate her too when she went her own way.

Forcing herself to believe Juan had given them the tickets only to validate his marriage and keep his reputation in good standings, she separated from Crista and Bruce and hurried to her hotel room to get ready.

Twenty minutes later, she stood next to the fence line, front and center. Bundled in layers against the cold, she leaned against Crista for warmth while Bruce stood close behind them both to shield the wind from their backs.

Crista leaned in and shouted in her ear. "Do you see him yet?"

Dana shook her head, searching the base of the slope. Her stomach quivered. Watching the Olympics on television, from the comfort of her home, hadn't prepared her for the onslaught of nerves hitting her now. She knew Juan. She'd slept with him. Her husband was doing something that most people couldn't even imagine doing in their lifetime.

The first time she'd witnessed him skiing, the fear for his safety had overshadowed her awe of his talents. But she'd watched him practice, and he took the sport seriously. Dedicated and smart, he'd taken no chances. A few times, she'd even watched him walk away from the ramp because of unsafe conditions.

"There he is." Bruce shoved his arm between her and Crista, pointing up the hill.

In a blue suit with white stripes, Juan was merely a dot on the hillside. Dana accepted the binoculars Bruce handed her. She peered up the slope. T.T. was on the ramp, and Juan stood off to the side, bouncing in place. His arms stretched in the air.

She wanted to stop looking, but she couldn't turn away. Whether Juan stood in front of her laughing or strutted around the hotel naked, he never failed to grab her attention. The same went for when he was in his zone. She found him irresistible.

The air horn sounded. She lowered the binoculars and gazed at the ramp. Her heart raced. The USA team was up. T.T. moved into position. She passed the binoculars to Bruce and grabbed Crista's hand. This was so exciting.

The next signal blasted. She stared intently as T.T. moved, afraid to blink in case she missed anything. One second he was speeding down the ramp, and the next he was in the air. She gasped, barely taking in the twists of his airborne body, and he landed.

T.T.'s left leg slid out to the side, and he was down. Dana gasped, leaning forward. But before she could worry, he was sliding to a stop and raising his arm in a show that he was all right. Everything seemed to happen within a few seconds, and then his event was over.

"It's okay. He's okay. That was only the first run. He has two more." She ripped the binoculars out of Bruce's hand. "Oh my God. Juan's up."

Crista took the binoculars. "He better win, or I'm going to slug him. I have a thousand bucks in the pool saying he'll come in first."

"What?" She glanced at Crista before looking back at Juan. "You're betting on the outcome?"

"Don't worry, we all put money on him, but I bought the top square," Crista lowered her arm. "Six grand to the winner. It would've been seven, but we couldn't talk Diana into giving us any of her money. That girl thinks splurging on a thirty-dollar pair of sneakers is wasting money despite having a boyfriend who was more than willing to loan her enough to buy a square. Hell, even Shauna pitched in."

"Seven is Juan's lucky number and the one I ordered put on his suit," Dana said.

The first warning boom went off behind them. She jumped, turning to Crista. "Count me in. I'll pay you when I get back to the hotel room. I don't care what square, but Juan needs all the luck he can get."

Crista put her arm around Dana's waist. "I knew I liked you."

The discharge shot rocked the area. The time clock started. Juan pushed off the launching pad.

Dana's focus centered on her husband. Her whole body shut down. Breathing in air escaped her capabilities. Numbness froze her to any movement and touch. The only thing she absorbed was the growing *shhh* from the cut of Juan's skis, as he grew closer to the edge of the ramp.

Juan crouched, tucking his poles, and lifted. His body horizontal with the ground, he soared. Dana's eyes burned from the cold, but she refused to blink. As if suspended in air, Juan twisted once, twice, three times.

Then he was falling. Dana screamed inside, though she wasn't aware of moving an inch or hearing any noise. The crowd had grown deathly quiet, and everyone held their breath, waiting for Juan to touch ground.

Then, after what seemed like the longest five seconds of her life, Juan landed. Dana's throat closed. Cheers deafened her, and she finally recuperated enough to sag against the fence.

"Sonofabitch, he did it," Bruce yelled. "Did you see that? Near flawless dismount."

She understood perfectly what Juan had accomplished. Adrenaline surged, and she clapped, giving her best that's-my-man scream. He'd pushed his way into first place going into the second round.

Ten feet away, Juan skied to the fence. He smiled for the camera, stopping to say a few words to the reporters who held microphones over the barrier. All over the world, viewers would hear what Juan's first reaction was over his impeccable jump. They'd celebrate with him.

One woman worked her way to the front. Dana leaned forward, watching her progress. The woman grabbed the front of Juan's jacket and pulled him closer, until Juan leaned over the fence.

The woman, head to toe in a red snowsuit, looking fabulous with her puffed out hair and bright red lipstick, then threw her arms around Juan's neck and kissed him on the mouth. Dana's heart sank when Juan pulled out of the kiss and raised his arm in victory.

The crowd ate him up. They loved him, and he obviously appreciated their support.

Dana's heart pounded, and the energy from moments ago fled. Heavy hearted and banned from being with him, she couldn't help feeling like the third wheel.

She wanted to be the person congratulating him.

She wanted to share in his excitement.

She wanted to be the only woman to kiss him in celebration.

Instead, she turned around and spoke to Crista. She wasn't aware of what she said to make her excuses, but Crista and Bruce let her leave alone to go back to the hotel. She'd seen enough for the day.

Chapter Nineteen

The only thing pushing Juan toward the hotel room after midnight was the thought that he'd see Dana. Weary and exhausted, he couldn't wait to catch up with her and unwind. He'd barely had five minutes to himself all day, and the adrenaline rush from the event had plummeted an hour ago.

Every country wanted an interview. There were translators to wait for, autographs to sign, and Coach Lindhurst to deal with. Talk about on the edge. All he wanted to do is collapse in bed and hold Dana to his chest.

If he heard Coach lecture one more time about his behavior—after being the model athlete—he'd break out a six-pack and chug them all down in front of him. The hell with the baggage of being in front of the public. He wanted to ski.

That's all he ever focused on. Skiing came first. He paused outside the hotel door. At one time, he'd flourished under the attention from the fame.

Dana changed everything for him. It wasn't the crowd and excitement that had boosted him today; it was winning for Dana. Skiing was a whole other event, knowing he not only wanted to win, but he wanted to impress his wife because she was watching and expecting him to do well.

He removed the keycard from the pocket of his jacket, slid it through the slot, and opened the door. The Olympics had become about more than just winning the gold the day he'd stripped Dana out of her wedding dress. This year, he wanted to win his wife.

He flipped on the light, threw his duffle toward the wall, and walked across the room. Halfway to the bedroom, he stopped and turned around. Warmth flooded him. Dana slept curled in the corner of the couch.

Still clothed, with her jacket covering her shoulders, she had her hand tucked under her cheek. He strolled over and squatted beside her, noticing she'd kicked off her boots at least. She'd had a busy day.

From the rumors circulating, Reese Company was the showcased skiwear company this year. Although he'd had no doubt she'd succeed in landing new contracts, he also knew how hard she worked for her father. But he hoped her stint working in her family's business would come to an end tomorrow.

He wanted her to have everything she desired, and working for Colton Reese put a weight on her shoulders, holding her back from achieving her dream.

"Babe?" he whispered.

She wiggled deeper into the couch. He brushed the piece of soft hair out of the corner of her mouth. She was exhausted. Tomorrow would be an even bigger day, and she needed her rest.

The toll of doing business and trying to keep up with his schedule had caught up with her. He leaned closer and kissed the end of her nose. She'd supported him, not only emotionally, but would rub his back and pamper him when he dragged himself inside the hotel every evening.

He picked her up, groaning when his shoulder protested the movement. Today's runs had gone smoothly, and the only thing he could think of that would be causing his shoulder to act up was the stress he was under, the constant tension. Nothing that a little ice wouldn't help, but it gave him one more thing to worry about.

Dana snuggled her face against the crook of his neck. His whole body calmed and today slipped away. This was where he wanted to be. Right here. Holding his wife.

He laid her in the bed, kissed her nose, and walked back out into the kitchen. He put some ice in a Ziploc bag, and returned to the bedroom. Too tired to strip out of his clothes, he kicked off his shoes and collapsed on the bed, laying the cold pack on his shoulder.

Dana rolled over and threw her arm across his middle. He stroked her hair as he closed his eyes. His life had changed directions when she told him she was leaving. He'd panicked, thinking she'd walk away from him and he'd never see her again.

He'd used the only excuse he had to make sure she came to Germany. Her commitment to her father and the Reese Company never wavered during their time together. Her own life in turmoil, she always put her commitments and responsibilities first. He relied on that redeeming quality of Dana's to buy himself more time with her.

A month spent together wasn't enough time to fall in love. That was what he'd told himself whenever he started to let himself think of her more than a temporary wife. He even had himself convinced that what they were experiencing was a flirtationship.

But the threat of losing her scared him to death. He was no longer fooling around. He'd fallen in love somewhere between her wearing his sweatshirt and her failed attempt to seduce him with the worst toddies he'd ever had. And, because Dana had made them, he'd drunk the whole thing just so she'd smile.

Tomorrow, he'd let her know that he was in love with her.

He yawned. Tomorrow, he'd do things the right way. The way Dana deserved, and needed. Then when the Olympics ended and he stood upon the gold medalist platform, Dana would be his wife in the true sense of the matter. And only then would he achieve *his* dream.

Chapter Twenty

The phone rang. Juan jolted awake and looked at the clock. *Shit.*

He'd slept the whole night.

Dana removed her leg from over his. He hardened, wanting the time to make love to her and knowing he couldn't. His second event was today. If he nailed his scores, he'd seal his spot on a platform. If he screwed up, he'd have to fight for his life in the final event and there was always a chance that one of the other guys would have three average runs, pushing him out of his position.

"What time is it?" Dana snuggled down into the covers.

"Five in the morning." He rolled out of bed and stood. "I feel like I could sleep all day."

"Jet lag." She lifted her head. "And maybe that whole thing about you kicking ass on the slopes in the freaking Olympics."

He laughed. "Yeah, that might have something to do with being tired."

"Smart and sexy." She stretched and rolled onto her back. "No wonder women throw themselves at you. They see the perfect man who can charm, ski like a boss, and can bring them a secure life if they rope the Olympian. You're the whole package and you come with your own poles … and goggles."

He stilled. "Goggles are important?"

"They are when they come from the Reese Company," she said, pulling the blanket up. "God, it's cold in here."

He groaned and looked at her. Rumpled, her hair spread over the surface of the pillow, she presented a temptation he wasn't sure if he could walk away from, even when the gold was at stake. He wanted to crawl under the covers with her, and warm her up.

He ran his hands over his face. "I need to get downstairs for a press conference, but it shouldn't last very long. Then I'll be able to come back and spend an hour or so with you before I have to prep for today's event."

"Don't worry about that, I'm going to be busy myself." Dana slid out of bed, wrapping the sheet around her body, despite being fully clothed. "I'm going to grab a hot shower. I have two meetings this morning. You can come back and have the suite to yourself and rest. It's important that you catch as many catnaps as you can to gather your energy. You wouldn't want to wear yourself out."

"Hey." He tagged her waist and dragged her back against him. "Everything okay?"

"Sure." She pulled away from him. "Just trying to get business done before I go watch your second event."

"You're sure?" He studied her. "You seem kind of distant."

She shrugged. "I told you, we're suffering from jet lag. I crashed last night. It makes me feel disconnected and groggy."

He cupped her face. "I don't like you not feeling well. Can I get you a couple Tylenol or a coffee?"

"No, but thanks." Her smile never reached her eyes and she patted his chest. "I better get ready."

She'd snubbed him. He walked around the bedroom, not understanding what had happened. It was as if Germany had invaded their lives, and Dana now avoided any form of intimacy with him. Hell, she hadn't even spoken to him about how he'd done yesterday or pointed out anything that would help him in the next event like she usually did. When he'd finally worked his way over to where he knew Bruce and Crista were standing with her yesterday, Dana had left.

Yet she told him how perfect and smart and sexy he was? He shook his head. Now that he thought about it, she wasn't teasing him the way she usually did. She was serious. He let his chin drop to his chest and he stared at the bedspread falling off the bed. She'd turned his talent into an insult. He wasn't a sex object.

Dana came back out of the bathroom. "I forgot, but your mom wanted me to tell you she loves you and she's crossing her fingers and toes for you."

He scratched his chest. "I was busy yesterday and meant to find her and Maria. I told them they'd be better to watch from home, but Mom was determined to come and support me."

Dana frowned. "She's proud of you. It's important to her to be here and show the world her support. You can't deny her that."

He nodded. "I know. I wish I had more time to connect with them while I'm here, but I can't even find time to have breakfast with them or you. I feel bad. I've neglected you and I really want—"

"Juan?" Dana stared at the floor beside the bed. "Why is there an ice bag on the floor?"

Her whole body stiff, she swung her gaze in his direction. He moved to the bed, and swept the bag up.

"It's nothing," he said, walking out of the room and tossing the bag in the sink.

When he returned, Dana hadn't moved from her position in the room. She raked her teeth over her bottom lip. "Did you hurt your shoulder again?"

"No." He grabbed his shoulder and swung his arm, showing her he was perfectly fine. "I iced it last night as a precaution."

She stepped closer, frowning. "You're worried."

To distract her, he changed the subject. "I'm worried about us."

She flinched. He took in her reaction and knew he wasn't misunderstanding her attitude toward him. Something was definitely wrong, and he couldn't figure it out. They'd gotten along fabulously back in the States.

He hooked her finger and tugged her closer. "I think we need to talk."

"I need to go get ready," she muttered, pulling away from him.

"Wait." He gazed up at the ceiling, hoping he would say the right thing. "Just ... hang in there with me, babe."

She tilted her head. The little line between her brows deepened. He approached her and lifted her chin. "I know with everything going on it can get crazy, and the weird hours with us coming and going, not really having time to connect is taking its toll on you, me, and everyone."

"You have to concentrate—"

"I know, dammit." He inhaled deeply. "Please, give me time. I just need more time."

She gazed at his chest and nodded. "You better go, or you'll be late."

"I promise you. When I have time, we'll talk." He leaned down and kissed the tip of her nose. "I'll hurry through this morning's events, so try to take a break and meet me here in a couple of hours, okay?"

"I don't—"

"Babe ... " he whispered. "It's important. Meet me in the room in two hours."

"I'll try," she said.

Dana slipped away and closed the bathroom door. He sighed. How could he be on the top of his game competition wise, and have his life in the shitter?

He glanced at the clock, and hustled to change his clothes. He ran his hands through his hair and hurried out of the suite. Whatever the reporters asked him, he'd give short yes and no answers. Then he'd tell them what they wanted to hear when they asked what he was going to do first chance he got when the Olympics were over. Maybe he'd shock them all by skipping Disneyland and letting them know he was going straight to bed with his wife, because that's what he really wanted to do.

Chapter Twenty-One

"You're very welcome." Dana shook Mr. Kamachu's hand. "I'll be sure to send a sample of our newest style of jacket that Mr. Santiago wore yesterday to your main office. Also, because we at Reese Company stand behind our loyal customers, I'll throw in the female version as a gift."

She smiled as the biggest leader in outdoor wear in China walked away. Shutting her laptop, she slipped the computer into her bag. She was done with business for the duration of the Olympics. With half the winter events over, and only the skiing events left, she'd stopped taking appointments for her remaining time in Germany to be there to support Juan.

Ana, bundled from head to toe in the baby blue with winter white trim Reese outfit Dana had given her before reaching Germany as a thank you gift for welcoming her into the family, approached her. "There you are. I tried calling your room, but you'd already left. I wanted to invite you to breakfast."

"I'm sorry." Dana rubbed Ana's arm. "I had early appointments, and grabbed a pastry from downstairs. How are you enjoying Germany?"

"It's lovely. There is so much snow, but I'm warm and everyone is being so nice. I met T.T.'s mother and father, and they've invited me to dinner tonight. Do you think you and Juan will have time to join us too?" Ana asked.

"I'll ask, but his event time is later today. He's one of the last to go, so he probably won't have time with all the prep it takes before the he's called out on the slope." Dana clutched her bag, wanting to change the subject. "Where's Maria?"

"Denmark." Ana rolled her eyes.

Dana grinned, trying not to laugh. "She better watch out, or those boys from Denmark are going to pack her in one of their suitcases and take her home when the games are over."

Ana made the sign of the cross, and shook her head. "She needs to settle down, find a good man the way you did with my Juan. She's too wild."

Dana squeezed Ana's hand. "Your daughter is perfect. I don't think you have anything to worry about. Some lucky man will fall madly in love with her. She's wonderful."

"I hope so." Ana hugged her. "I'm going to go upstairs and take a nap, so I'll be ready for Juan's event."

"Okay. I'll see you later." Dana kissed her cheek.

Ana walked away, stopped, and turned back around. "Is everything okay?"

"Sure." She smiled. "Why?"

Ana's eyes softened. "I don't know. Call it mother's intuition, but you have a sadness to you."

She shook her head. "Just tired. All the excitement and dealing with Reese Company is harder than I thought. Plus, I'm nervous. I want Juan to achieve his dream."

"You and me both, sweetheart," Ana said. "You should rest too."

"I will." Dana picked up her other bag and waited until Ana disappeared into the elevator.

She had no idea how she'd face Ana when the truth came out about her faux marriage to her son. She'd grown to love the woman in the short time they'd spent together, and knew she'd hurt everyone she'd come to love when they arrived back in the States. She didn't want to lose Ana and Maria from her life.

Dana inhaled deeply, tossed her hair over her shoulder, and made her way to the elevator. Suddenly, an annulment was starting to feel too much like a divorce for her to be able to walk away without feeling a load of guilt. She and Juan were not the only ones involved anymore—they had family and mutual friends that were also going to be hurt.

A man bent over a self-serve newspaper dispenser outside the elevator, refilling it with the morning copies. She glanced at the headline and stopped. A picture of Juan smiling for the camera had hit the front page. She cleared her throat. "Could I have one of those, please?"

The man stood, nodded, and held out the bundle.

She dug out three euros out of her front pocket, not sure of the exchange or price. "You can keep the change."

He smiled and passed her the paper. She read the beginning of the article as she waited and then rode the elevator up to her floor. Once she walked out onto the third level, she snorted. Despite Juan being newly married, they still referred to him as Amante Español.

If only they knew how he hated the name.

She shoved the paper under her arm, and rearranged her bags so she could remove her key card from her pocket. She unlocked the door and walked in, dumping her things on the floor. Ana was right. Maybe a nap would snap her out of feeling sorry for herself and get her mind off of Juan.

She walked straight to the bedroom. It wasn't until she stopped to kick off one of her shoes that she realized she wasn't alone. Juan stood with his back to her in front of the bed, his shirt off, his hair a beautiful mess, and the corded muscles on his back looking drool-worthy. Her gaze dropped to the mattress, and all the air in the room disappeared.

A woman, lying on *her* pillow, in nothing but a slinky piece of black lingerie sat up in surprise. Dana couldn't take her eyes off her, because she couldn't believe there was a freaking woman in *her* bed.

Juan slowly turned around, saw Dana, and muttered, "Fuck."

She stared at him in disbelief, numb and shocked. He'd taken another women to bed. He'd known she was going to be away from the suite this morning.

"Babe ... it's not what it looks like." Juan stepped toward her.

She backed away, and bumped into the open door. "Don't."

"Dana. Let me—"

"No." She shook her head and whispered, "Don't say anything."

Not able to stay in the same room as Juan and that woman any longer, she ran out into the main part of the suite, grabbed her purse, and left the hotel room. In the hallway, she searched for somewhere to go.

She was in Germany. She had nowhere to go.

If she tried to make sense of what she'd seen inside the bedroom, she'd only end up making a fool of herself. She walked away and continued distancing herself from her nightmare. She continued to the stairs, and headed down. The sight of Juan and that woman fresh in her mind, she could only keep moving to try to escape from the truth.

She wasn't the only woman in Juan's life. There were always his fans. Fans willing to do anything to get a piece of the Olympic star. God, he'd fooled her for a month, thinking she was the center of his universe.

But she should've known. He kissed someone else after his first event. The press hounded him constantly. He was Amante Español.

Panic hit her as she pushed her way out to the main floor. She doubled at the waist, unable to inhale. Her chest squeezed, holding the sob in, and she freaked. Spots littered her vision and she leaned against the wall.

Bruce walked through the door, spotted her, and grabbed her before she sunk to the floor. "Dana, shit, what's wrong?"

She patted her throat and shook her head. "I-I c-ca ... "

He swept her up into his arms. "I'll take you to your room, and call an ambulance."

She shook her head, and fought him. "N-no."

"Okay." He murmured words that she couldn't understand.

Her life exploded, and she didn't want Juan seeing her like this. She wanted to go home, and get as far away from him and that woman as she could. God, she was so stupid.

"Talk to me, sweetheart." Bruce carried her up the stairs. "Are you hurt?"

She buried her head in his neck and shook her head. Yes, she hurt all over, but mostly in her heart.

"Good ... good." Bruce shifted her, and opened the door. "Almost to my room, hang in there."

She tightened her hold on his shoulders. Bruce was big enough to hide her from the world. The world that would look at her and know that Juan had cheated on her.

In Bruce's hotel room, he set her on the couch. "Crista!"

Dana wrapped her arms around her waist and leaned forward, rocking. She wanted to erase the last five minutes. She wanted to scrub her mind clean of seeing Juan with that woman. She moaned, forcing herself not to cry. This was her fault.

She'd talked Juan into marrying her. Her father had paid him to take her. He needed her to compete.

Crista rushed to her side and gathered her in her arms. "What happened?"

Dana closed her eyes, thankful for someone here who'd hold her. If only someone could make everything better. She sucked at fixing her life. How was she going to get out of this mess? How was she supposed to stop loving someone?

"I found her like this downstairs. I asked her if she needed help, and then she flipped out when I told her I'd take her back to her room." Bruce held out a glass of water.

Dana ignored the drink. Bruce picked up her hand, and set the glass in her grasp.

"Drink. It's vodka … it's all I could find. It'll help you breathe and calm down," he said.

Crista forced her to take a sip. She coughed, but once she stopped, a comforting warmth filled her chest and eased the tightness. She lifted the glass again. The next swallow was easier to handle.

"T-thanks." She inhaled a choppy breath.

"Did someone hurt you?" Crista rubbed her back.

She stared at the floor and nodded. The only person who had the ability to wound her to the core had. She always protected herself. Being Colton Reese's daughter meant she guarded her feelings and never let another person's actions or words affect her.

But she'd let Juan into her life, and there was no stopping him. He'd romanced, played, and fooled her. She'd let him know her dreams, and allowed herself to be real for the first time in her life. Before she'd known what was happening, she'd forgotten they were only pretending.

"Do you want me to see if I can find Juan?" Crista asked.

"No." Dana inhaled deeply, and took another sip. "I never want to see him again."

"Shit." Bruce ran his hand through his hair. "This is not good. He has an event he needs to concentrate on."

"Shut up." Crista glared at him. "Can't you see she's upset because of something Juan did to her?"

She glanced at Crista. "That's not true. It's my fault."

Crista stiffened. Dana scooted back and pressed into the couch. These were Juan's friends. She had no right to bother them.

"I know your loyalty is with Juan." She drank more from the cup, because right now that was the only thing making her feel a little bit better. "Just let me sit here for a few minutes, and then

I'll leave. I'll figure out what I'm supposed to do and where I need to go."

Bruce moved and sat on the coffee table in front of her. "You're not going anywhere. Whether you had a fight with Juan or not, you can't go wandering around Germany by yourself without any protection."

"I really thought ... " She shuddered.

"What, sweetheart?" Bruce laid his hands on her knees. "What did you think?"

How could she answer the question? For the last month, she'd started to think that happiness was attainable to a person like her, and not everyone ended up like her parents. That she didn't have to settle for compatibility and a smart business plan, but could let herself find love. True love, the kind other people found.

She'd even second-guessed her stupid life schedule, and had decided to throw away her pre-conceived idea to follow a timeline for Juan's much more spontaneous life.

"I loved him," she whispered. "For the first time in my life, I wanted him more than anything else."

Crista held her hand. "What makes you think he doesn't have the same feelings?"

"I just do." She handed Bruce her empty glass. "Would you mind if I had a little more?"

Bruce glanced at Crista, who shrugged. "Sure. I'll be right back."

Once Bruce left the room, Dana turned to Crista. "I know you're friends with Juan, but as a woman, please understand I'm not going to hurt him. I just need to leave."

"But what happened?" Crista frowned.

"Amante Español happened," she said.

"No ... " Crista slouched on the couch. "He wouldn't."

"He totally did. I saw them." A shiver crawled up her spine. "She was in *my* bed, on *my* pillow, with *my* husband."

"I'll kill him," Crista muttered.

Calmer and stronger, Dana patted Crista's leg. "Let him finish the Olympics, and then you can do whatever you want to him. I'm done. I can't keep doing this."

Bruce returned with two glasses and passed one to Crista too, who readily shot all of hers down in one swallow before turning to Bruce. "Men are assholes."

"Shit," he mumbled. "Then you're really going to be pissed when you find out I called—"

The door burst open, slamming against the wall. Juan stood in the room, shirtless, frazzled, and staring intently at Dana.

Without missing a beat, Dana chugged her second glass of vodka back in one shot. Maybe he'd disappear and she wouldn't feel like rushing into his arms and begging him to take her back.

"Come on, we're going to our room and talking." Juan marched toward her.

"No thanks." She eyed the empty glass and frowned. "I've overstayed my month, our fake marriage is over. So is our flirtationship."

"What?" Bruce asked.

"Oh, shit," Crista whispered, shaking her head.

Dana, for the first time since they'd started the stupid charade to fool everyone, felt like talking. "It all started when I got stood up at the altar by a guy named Jace. Totally screwed up my life schedule. I was devastated … and pissed. Juan showed up and helped me strip out of my wedding dress—God, such a waste. It was beautiful and lacy with a deep scoop, baring my back. My dream dress—and then I used my mouth on his zipper, and … "

She smiled as she kept talking. It really was an interesting story when she thought about it. She looked around the room, blinking to stop the room from spinning. Crista and Bruce stared at her in fascination. Juan glared at her. Determined to come clean, she continued.

She wasn't aware of when she stopped talking and Juan started. His voice lulled her into a comfortable place, and Bruce's couch was really cushy. She closed her eyes and listened.

Chapter Twenty-Two

Juan paced the room, ignoring the time. In a half hour, he was supposed to be at a team meeting to pick up his time slot for tonight. Then he was to go immediately to the slope for the second of three events. By the end of tonight, he'd know the outcome of where he placed.

"She's waking up," Crista whispered.

Juan rushed to the couch. Dana yawned, looking around the room.

No matter how many times he'd ordered everyone to leave, his friends and family had set up camp, determined to help. He wanted no one's help. He wanted his wife to believe him, and look at him as if he could do no wrong.

Earlier in Bruce's room, he'd relayed the story of the woman in the bed until he couldn't think of another thing to say and when he was done, Dana was conked out on the couch oblivious to what really happened. Damn Bruce for thinking a drink would fix Dana's problem.

Like vodka would straighten out his life, and get his wife back. She couldn't even handle a hot toddy—of course two cups of vodka on top of jet lag would put her right to sleep.

"Babe?" He sat on the coffee table and stroked Dana's arm. "Can you wake up, and listen?"

She blinked at him. He saw the moment everything came back to her, because she moved fast to get off the couch and away from him. He held her in place.

"Listen to me for a second. It's time for me to leave, but that woman ... I don't know who she was." Juan brought her face around when she looked away. "I was in the bathroom, going to jump in the shower, and I heard the door open. I thought it was you. I hurried to finish washing, because I wanted to talk to you and find out what was going through your head the last several days. But when I went into the bedroom, I found the woman in our bed. You came in right afterward. Nothing happened," he said.

Dana stared at him. "I have a headache."

"Yeah. I bet you do. You can thank Bruce for that." He scowled at Bruce. "I talked with security while you were sleeping. They're going to put a security guard at the elevators, and make sure nobody without a pass makes it past the lobby. That should've been done to start with, but there will be no more fans allowed onto the upper floors without approval."

Dana frowned. "You really didn't know her?"

"Hell, no. You know me, babe. Have I given you one reason to doubt that I'm with you?" He moved over and sat beside her on the couch.

"No, but you are Amante Español. Women throw themselves at you. Like the woman after your event that kissed you. You never stopped her." She lifted her head at his mom's gasp. "Oh God, I told everyone what happened between us, didn't I?"

"Look at me." He hooked her neck and brought her eyes around to him. "I'm your Amante Español. Only yours."

Her chin trembled. "Everyone knows we're not … we aren't … that it's all fake."

He leaned his forehead against hers and chuckled softly. "Yeah."

"I probably shouldn't have done that," she whispered.

"It's okay. Bruce was the only one who hadn't heard. I'd already confessed to Mom and Maria. Crista knew from the start." he said.

She pulled back. "What? But they were so nice to me."

"They love you." He cleared his throat. "I'm sorry you had to come in our room and see that woman. I'd never bring someone to our room. I hope you know that."

She nodded. "I feel better knowing you weren't sneaking her by me when you knew I was working."

"Never," he said.

"I'm sorry I told everyone the truth." She kissed him softly. "Today sucks."

"Yeah, it does, but it's over. Right?" He waited for her to nod and kissed her again. "I hate to do this, but I need to leave. Will you be able to come to the second event?"

"Yeah." She inhaled deeply. "You better go."

He studied her, not wanting to leave. "Are we good?"

She nodded.

He whispered, "Promise?"

"Promise," she whispered back.

Dana seemed shaky, as if what he said wasn't soaking in. He stood, kissed his mom, and walked out of the hotel. He needed time for just Dana and him, and between now and the end of the games, he barely had time to eat, much less tell her he loved her in a way she'd remember for the rest of her life.

The next hour, he went from meeting to meeting, and finally he suited up for the second event. In the dressing room, he called Dana. "Hey, how are you feeling?"

"Better. Your mom, sister, and Crista made me eat, and that helped." She paused. "Are you nervous?"

"Not anymore." He lowered his voice. "You're going to watch me ski, right?"

"Of course," she said.

"Okay," he said on an exhale. "I better get ready."

"Juan, wait ... "

"Yeah?" He dropped his chin to his chest.

"Good luck," she said.

He smiled. "Thanks."

He disconnected the call. Feeling more positive that he managed to buy himself more time, he dressed in his Reese gear, and followed his manager outside to a waiting car, which would drive him five hundred yards to where he'd ride the chair up the mountainside.

The routine never changed, whether it was practice or the Olympics. He used the interval to meditate, to clear his mind, and relax all his muscles. He focused on the jump, imagining the entire run repeatedly in his mind until he could see how it'd turn out.

He rode the chair up the slope by himself, preferring solitude to a pep talk from his trainer. Today, he needed to put his mind at ease after a day of total chaos and facing his greatest fear.

He searched the crowd for Dana. She always wore her bright pink down jacket with the fur-lined hood covering her hair. Every time she wore the coat, he wanted grab hold of her and kiss her. He warmed. God, she was beautiful.

Just looking at her kept him satisfied, and he wanted to spend the remainder of his days gazing at her. The way she wrinkled her nose when she was irritated, or the way her eyes widened when she tried to hide her reaction when he touched her. He doubted he'd ever get bored spending the rest of his life with her. She simply fascinated him.

It'd killed him to see the hurt and disappointment on her face when she spotted the woman in their room. Who he was and what he did for a living had put her in that situation, and he took responsibility. He should've foreseen something like this happening, and made sure the hotel was secure enough to protect her.

He'd changed since he'd met her.

At the beginning of their plan to fool the coaches and the board into believing he'd given up his playboy lifestyle for married life, he thought he'd miss the women, the parties, and the attention. He hadn't. Not one tiny bit.

Despite the rumors, he was selective in his bed partners. He enjoyed a good time, but he preferred to know who he was sleeping with when he did decide to have sex.

The lift came to the end and began to loop, and he slid off the chair. Coach Lindhurst waited for him. He skied over to the waiting area.

"You're first up." Coach tapped his clipboard. "You've got the prime, headlining spot tonight to come in and win this thing. All you need to do is give a steady jump. Don't risk anything, because we can throw this score out. Make a solid landing, and you're in perfect position to bring home the gold."

"Got it," he said.

Coach slapped him on the back. "Focus."

"Right." He pushed away, and raised his arms above his head to stretch.

Keeping his muscles warm and loose, he jumped in place on his skis, constantly moving, and keeping his body ready. He ignored the other men coming up the lift. He'd ski, finish, and make his exit. No one expected him to wait around in the cold for the others to take their turn.

He had no desire to know where he placed. One of the coaches always called and kept him abreast of the results.

For him, skiing was an individual sport. He supported and cheered his teammates from the U.S. on, but when the scores came in, it was him against the clock. Exactly how he preferred it.

"Santiago to the platform," the announcer spoke over the speaker.

He skied over to the gate, and nodded at the guy manning the entrance. In precise steps, he climbed the platform and stood behind the flyaway gate that was remotely controlled by the clock. He rolled his head to each shoulder, loosening his neck muscles.

Then he studied the ramp. The first event on a clean surface came with advantages. He had a smooth entrance and he'd gain speed faster. But there was always the worry that his foot would slide. Because the other skiers' markings were absent, he could easily misjudge the jump point. Too early, and he wouldn't gain enough height. Too late, and he'd shoot too far.

He had to leave the ramp at the perfect spot, timing everything to the perfect dismount or risk injury to himself. He'd be lucky to walk away with a low score. Alpine skiing was an unforgiving sport. Precision meant everything.

Unaware that he'd even been looking, he spotted a pink splash among the red, white, and blue below the landing on the other side of the fence. Adrenaline fueled him and he knew without a doubt Dana had come to watch the way she'd promised.

He let his poles hang from his wrists, grabbed the railing, and slid back and forth, tracking the snow pack to give him enough traction and side support to push off. Once his tips tilted, he was on his own.

"Thirty seconds," the loudspeaker said.

He gripped the handles of his poles held them in front of him, points back, and forced himself to look away from Dana and eye the ramp. He would look neither down nor up, but straight ahead. From here on, his eyes stayed in front of him.

"Ten seconds. Set."

He crouched. His heart raced, but his muscles stayed loose. He'd done this a million times. It was time to fly.

Chapter Twenty-Three

The crowd was bigger, louder, and more tense than the last time Dana had stood at the fence, but she came prepared. The hot coffee in her gloved hands kept her warmer. The fact that Crista and Bruce acted as if she hadn't had a meltdown earlier or duped them into believing she was married for real helped her feel better.

She believed Juan was innocent, and he hadn't taken the woman to their room. The security guard promising to keep their suite safe enforced the emotional toll Juan went through when fans went to great depth to meet him. She wasn't the only one who'd been compromised. But Juan had come after her, and given her hope.

She'd heard something in his voice that made her believe there was something more he wanted to tell her. For that reason alone, she'd concluded that she had to tell him the truth the moment they both had time to talk more than five minutes.

She loved him.

Today was one of the worst days of her life. To believe, even for a short period, that Juan could forget about her so easily hurt. She didn't want to go on with her life wondering if things would end differently if she'd confessed to having fallen in love with him.

Even with the chance that Juan only saw her as a friend, and wanted the annulment in the end, at least she would have tried. Over the last month, she'd discovered a life schedule didn't mean much when the person in her life meant more to her than when she reached superficial goals that meant little to her but bragging rights.

She'd rather have a month with Juan than a marriage to Jace or any other guy. For her, Juan was the perfect man. He completed her. He made her feel safe and appreciated. She swallowed. No one had ever held her with such tenderness that tears blurred her vision, and she let herself rely on him.

Juan did all those things and much more for her, and he needed to know it.

"Juan's on the ramp," Bruce said.

She set her cup on the ground. Her hands shook, and she'd never be able to hold onto the coffee once Juan exited the gate.

"The wind is picking up," Crista said, holding onto the hood of her coat.

"Oh, God." Dana gulped. "Is there a way we can let him know?"

"He knows," Bruce said. "He's a pro. He's skied in worse conditions. He'll be fine."

"Juan will kick ass, just wait. He's great at feeling out the slope." Crista linked her arm with Dana. "Cross your fingers."

Dana couldn't even do that much with her gloves on, but she chanted Juan's name to herself. When the buzzer rent the air, she was prepared this time, though she swallowed air. Glued to the sight of Juan coming down the slope, she watched and waited. She had no idea if he was going too fast or too slow, she only soaked him in.

He was the picture perfect example of an athlete. Motivating, captivating, and inspiring. She'd never get used to how sexy he was on the snow and off the mountain. She stretched as Juan came off the ramp and flew. He twisted once, twice, and the rear of his skis crossed, stopping his motion. She gasped, shaking her head, wanting to deny what was happening, but she'd seen it.

One miniscule mistake. Whether it was the wind, or bad timing, Juan couldn't pull into the turn. Then he descended, and fear flooded her mind.

He landed skis first and careened to his side, flipping and turning. The snow billowed into the air, blocking him from view as he tumbled down the side of the mountain. She pushed forward, but the fence held her back. "Juan!" she screamed.

"Fuck," Bruce muttered, wrapping his arms around her from behind and pulling her away.

She fought him. "Let me go!"

"Sweetheart, the rescue team is already on him. Let's get back to the medi-center. Then we'll wait to find out what happened. There's nothing we can do for him. We'd only get in the way of the doctors. Let the professionals take care of him. He's got the best team looking out for him." Bruce tugged her along.

She stumbled, glancing over her shoulder, needing to see Juan. A fall at that speed could —

"Dammit, don't go there, girl." Crista grabbed her other arm. "He'll be all right. It's Juan we're talking about. He's tough and stubborn."

Outside the medi-center trailer, Dana spotted Ana and Maria. She broke free and ran toward them. She huddled them both in her arms, absorbing their cries as they worried about their son and brother.

"Stay strong," Dana whispered. "He'll be fine."

"They took him out on a stretcher," Juan's mom said, wiping her face with her glove. "There was nothing I could do to protect him."

"He's strong and he knows what to do if something goes wrong, right?" Dana rubbed Ana's back through her heavy coat. "He'll be fine."

"Do you think they'll let us in to see him?" Maria moved over closer to Ana, and took her mom's hand.

"I don't know what they do ... Juan never talked about what would happen if ... " Dana blew out her cheeks. "We'll wait. If someone comes out, we'll ask how we gain clearance. That's all we can do is wait and be positive."

Her stomach flip-flopped, and she gazed at Crista for guidance. Dana had no idea how they ran things here and apparently Crista didn't have a clue either, because she shook her head.

Waiting to hear if Juan was even in the building or if they'd taken him straight to the hospital was the only thing they could do. She rubbed Ana's free hand, keeping her warm. Juan's mother shook from fear, and it wouldn't do her any good to make herself sick.

"He'll be okay," Dana repeated again, to remind herself not to jump to conclusions. "That's what we all have to believe."

Ana nodded. "He will. I know he will. Juan's a good man. He's worked hard his whole life for this moment."

"Hell, yeah," Bruce mumbled. "He's in top shape. He'll be fine."

Thankful to have everyone around her, Dana knew Juan had to be okay. He had too many people who loved and cared about him. Too many people pulling for him.

"I'm going to call Shauna. She can call the others and let them know what's going on. I don't want her, Grayson, Dominic, and Diana to hear about this on the news." Crista walked off and made the phone call in private.

Seconds turned into minutes, and even supported by Juan's people, the longer Dana waited the more desperate the situation seemed. She needed to see Juan, to touch him, to brush his hair off his forehead and trace the white scar on his eyebrow that he got when he was ten and fell riding a skateboard. She wanted to make sure he was warm and comfortable. If he was hurting, she could make him laugh and forget about the pain.

How many times had she amused him without even trying? She sniffed. She'd give anything to hold his hand right now.

She closed her eyes to keep the tears at bay. Desperate for him to be okay, she'd beat him to the lawyer and get an annulment first thing, if it would guarantee that he was all right.

The door opened on the trailer, and a man wearing a blue suit stepped outside. His mouth was set, and there was no emotion in his eyes. "Dana Santiago?"

She jumped. "Me. Right here."

The man motioned her over. She squeezed Ana's hand before hurrying toward the door.

"Come in." The man stepped back and held the door open for her.

Dana stood at the threshold. "Are you sure you weren't asking for Juan's mother? I can get—"

"No, Mrs. Santiago. Your husband gave explicit instructions that he wanted you." The man laid his hand on her shoulder and urged her through the door.

She stood inside, searching for Juan, but he was nowhere in sight. The man walked past her, pointing for her to follow. She stuck to his back. In another area, she heard a man's deep voiced cussing, and the relief was so swift and deep, she grabbed onto the person who had come for her.

"He's right in here, ma'am," he said.

"Thank you." She stepped inside.

Juan sat on a gurney, a scowl on his face. She scanned his whole body, making sure he still had all his legs and arms. Finally, her gaze landed on the icepack bandaged to his shoulder. Her heart sank. He'd hurt his arm again.

Juan continued to argue with the two men in the room without looking at her. She approached the bed, and hooked her finger with Juan's finger.

He turned his head, noticing her for the first time, and blurted, "I'm fine."

"That's good to know," she whispered, glad to see him sitting, talking, and arguing.

For a while there, she'd imagined the worst while waiting to find out what happened after she saw him go down. She wasn't sure she'd survive if something happened to him.

"They want me to pull out of the last event." His mouth hardened. "I'm going to ski."

She moistened her lips. "Your shoulder?"

"A little swelling and stiffness, but it's okay." He lifted her arm, showing her. "I can work around it. I've done it before, and I can do it now. My final run is in an hour. I have to compete."

A man with gray hair moved closer. "He's irritated his rotary cuff on the site where he had surgery nine months ago. The swelling won't go down without steroids. Of course, he's refusing a shot, because it'll disqualify him from competing. As a doctor, I'd recom—"

"I'm skiing." He stood, winced, and struggled to put his good arm into his polyurethane unibody suit.

"Juan … " Dana put her hands on his stomach. "Maybe you should listen to him."

"No." He pulled his arm fully into the suit and left his injured arm out. "Nothing is going to stop me from my last run."

"But Juan … " She stroked his face. "It's your body. You only have one, and you don't want to further damage your shoulder."

Her words meant nothing to him. He'd never back down from a challenge, because that was the type of man she'd fallen in love with. He took care of himself, and her. She sighed. Proud to a fault.

"I need to do this. If I quit now it'll haunt me for the rest of my life. I have plans, and those plans don't involve forfeiting. I'm not a quitter, and I'm not going to start now. I won't go out this way." He stared at her intently.

Worry and fear flooded her, but there was something else making her stand on her tiptoes to kiss him. "Okay, honey. Let's get you ready to win."

His chin lifted, and he grabbed her hand. His grasp was almost painful, but right now, she needed that reassurance that he was okay. He led her through the trailer and outside, where he was swarmed by his family and friends. She stood back, as far as his grip on her would allow, and let him calm everyone down and reassure them that he was okay. The relief on everyone's faces brought tears to hear eyes.

He was loved. Not only by those who knew him well, but by everyone back in United States waiting to see if their superstar would compete. He was more than their chance at bringing home the gold. He validated that hard work, dedication, and never giving up would pay off to achieving their dream.

"You're really okay?" Ana patted him all over, including tenderly poking the arm that hung out of his ski suit.

"I'm good, Mom." Juan kissed his mom's cheek. "Stop worrying."

"We better get inside, and find you a new suit," Dana said.

She was shaking, whether from nerves or the frigid temperatures she didn't know, but she did know Juan must be freezing. Only half dressed with his bare arm hanging out of his suit, he appeared oblivious to the cold. She looped her arm around his waist and smiled at the others.

"Save me a spot by the fence. I'll hurry back after I make sure Juan's delivered safely to the dressing room and gets a new suit," she said.

Crista approached Juan. "I called Shauna, she filled in everyone else. They all want me to send you their best and tell you to kick ass."

Juan leaned over and kissed Crista's cheek. "That's the plan."

"And I have good news." Crista clasped her hands in front of her and grinned. "When I called, they were all at the hospital. Shauna is in labor. She's doing great, no problems at all. Grayson is driving her nuts and asking her every few seconds if she's okay, but Dominic is there to manhandle him. Diana is coaching her through contractions. They said someone would call me as soon as they have any news."

Juan's face softened and he smiled. "Sweet. A baby in our group."

Dana stood hypnotized by the change in Juan. His body relaxed and the smile came from his heart.

Juan waved off the person on the ATV waiting to drive them to the lodge. She and Juan moved together to take the walk together. She was determined to not let him out of her sight until it was absolutely necessary.

"Are you sure you don't want to ride?" she asked. "You're barely dressed."

He shook his head. "I need to walk to keep the stiffness from settling in, and the cold will do my shoulder good."

Regardless, she kept her arm around him and made sure he walked slowly. Maybe she was greedy, but she wasn't ready to watch him attempt another jump. It was one thing to attempt the ramp while in top shape, another when he was coming back from a fall and a hurt shoulder. She needed this time with him. Any sign that he had second thoughts, and she'd stand beside him and support any decision he made.

"That's good news about your friend having a baby." She glanced up at him. "Are you planning on going and seeing them when the games are over?"

"Eventually." He pulled her closer into his side. "You'd like them. Grayson and Shauna are … they're perfect. They deserve all the happiness a baby will bring into their life."

She refrained from replying. She had no idea if she'd get a chance to meet them, because Juan hadn't expressed any interest in talking about what would happen after the Olympics.

They reached the lodge door, and Juan dropped her hand and reached for the door. She stepped in front of him. "Can you wait a minute? I need to tell you something."

"Can't it wait until afterward?" he asked.

She swallowed, knowing it was now or never. If Juan was brave enough to get back up on the mountain and fly through the air on skis, she could tell him the truth. "No. It's important."

"Didn't I promise you that we'll talk later?" He ran the back of his fingers over her cheek. "I'm not going anywhere. You'll have lots of time to tell me whatever it is that's bothering you."

She captured his hand and put his fingers between her gloves, rubbing warmth into them. "You did, but I need to tell you something and I can't wait. I don't want to tell you afterward, because you'll be busy and I'll go ... "

"Babe ... " He squeezed her hand.

"I love you," she blurted.

Juan hooked her neck and brought her forward. He kissed her lips, her cheeks, her nose, and pulled back. "I know."

She waited expectantly for some kind of validation that he was feeling the same thing, or she wasn't reading their relationship the wrong way, but he volunteered nothing more.

"Okay, well, we better get you inside and warmed." She stepped back, keeping her disappointment out of her voice.

Juan remained in front of the door. "Will you do me a favor?"

"Of course," she whispered.

"I haven't told anyone, but I want you to be the first to know." He stretched his lips over his teeth, and he gazed over to the left toward the slope.

Her heart raced. She hoped he'd tell her he loved her, and wanted to stay married. At the least, let her know he wanted to continue seeing her after the Olympics.

"What is it?" she said.

"This will be my last Olympics. After today, I'm done competing. My shoulder isn't going to take another fall, and my goals have changed since I first started the journey in downhill skiing." Juan paused and inhaled deeply. "Even my manager doesn't know I'm walking away from the sport after I win my second gold."

Shocked, she said the first thing that popped into her head. "Wow. Are you sure?"

He threw back his head and laughed. She frowned, wondering if his fall had given him a concussion. She found nothing amusing about him making such a drastic life decision.

"You're cute," he said, pulling her against his chest. "That's exactly what I needed from you, babe."

She blew the air she held in her lungs out. "I'm not trying to be funny. What about your goals, your time, your ... skiing is your whole life."

He shrugged. "I guess my incentives have changed the older I get. I can afford to do anything I want, and I'm ready to move on to the next stage of my life. Maybe you and your time tables have rubbed off on me, and made me think of my life schedule."

She frowned. "I'm not sure you should've listened. I've been thinking lately that I might be wrong planning my life in such an extreme level. So far, it's not all it's cracked up to be, and I've failed every step of the way."

He leaned forward and kissed her hard. "You haven't failed, and I don't want you to ever change."

"I don't understand you. You're not acting normal," she muttered. "I think you're delusional. Skiing is your life. It's the only thing you live for."

"You'll understand later. Right now, I want you to hitch a ride back to the slope, and hang out with everybody at the finish line." He kissed the tip of her nose. "I need to go get ready. I still have a chance of winning the gold if I jump a perfect score. I'm not off the platform yet."

He waited until she stepped in front of him and walked down the hallway. At the elevator, she looked back and found him watching her. His facial expression went soft and he lifted his chin. She inhaled sharply and stepped into the elevator.

Soon, Juan's life would change in a dramatic way. Tears fell, and no sound came from her. She let the stress and heartache out. Because after today, her life would change too.

She only knew without Juan, she wouldn't like the direction her life headed.

Chapter Twenty-Four

The sea of red, white, and blue ski suits dotted the side of the mountain as the U.S. men's downhill ski team and entourage took their position. With Juan and T.T. the only two skiers from the U.S. team going into the final event against Germany, Hungary, and one skier from Russia, even the other countries who were eliminated earlier on came to show their support. Fans in the designated area at the base of the slope held signs to show their support. Dana gawked. The support for Juan was staggering. There was no doubt that he was the favorite skier in the final event.

She wondered how Juan would cope walking away from all the fame and glory. The attention, the hero-worship, the motivational speeches were what he lived for. He downplayed the importance, but she'd witnessed the joys and excitement rush through him. He became invincible when he was in his element.

Ana stroked Dana's cheek, bringing her attention back. She smiled in understanding at the joy written all over Juan's mother's face. Ana had a right to be proud of her son.

"The wait is killing me." Crista bounced in place. "I don't care that they say the last skier has the spotlight and all the focus is on Juan. In the Ironman, it's best to be in front. I have no patience for this kind of dragged out tension. It's only making me nervous. Now I think I have to pee."

"Hold it, lil' Chihuahua. You'll miss when Juan wins the gold if you take a pit stop now." Bruce threw a snowball at Crista. "Have Dominic or Diana called yet?"

Crista kicked snow on Bruce. "Don't be stupid. I'd tell you if I heard anything. God, how long does it take to have a baby anyway?"

"Shauna's probably having all the billboards around Cottage Grove painted first, so everyone in town knows she's having Grayson's baby." Bruce grinned.

Crista laughed. "I hope so. The girl deserves all the attention after pining away from Grayson her whole life."

Dana listened curiously. She hadn't even met the others, but she was intrigued. From what Juan had said, Grayson and Shauna were destined for each other. She liked that thought, and often wondered if fate had made her run into Juan when she was escaping the humiliation of being stood up on her wedding day.

"Why is it taking so long?" Maria groaned. "They announced Juan to the platform ten minutes ago."

Dana strode to the fence. "Maybe they're having camera difficulties or one of the judges had a question."

"Still, I don't remember a delay the last time Juan competed in the Olympics," Maria said.

At that moment, Crista's phone rang. Dana turned, along with everyone else, to find out if the baby had come.

Crista frowned at the screen and answered. "Who is this?"

Dana glanced at Maria and raised her brows. Crista wasn't lying when she said she was losing her cool. She'd snapped at whoever was on the phone.

Crista glanced at Dana, and quickly turned around. Dana whistled under her breath and went back to watching the hillside. Any longer and she was going to join Crista and start complaining. It was as if they were drawing out the suspense on purpose.

"Hey, Dana," Crista said.

She glanced over her shoulder. "Yeah?"

"You need to turn on your phone," Crista shut off her phone and shoved it in the pocket of her coat.

"Why?" she asked.

Crista rolled her eyes. "Because I asked you to, that's why."

"That's silly. No one but my dad is going to call me here. He knows I'm busy all day with Juan. Besides, rates are terrible here." She turned back around.

"God, you're stubborn." Crista reached into Dana's pocket.

Dana raised her arms to get out of Crista's way as her friend assaulted her body. "What are you doing?"

"Getting your phone." Crista stuck her tongue out the corner of her mouth. "Shit, girl. How much Kleenex do you need to carry with you?"

"For your information, those are for Juan. He always needs to wipe his goggles when he practices." Dana laughed when Crista pulled her coat off her hip and felt around for the pocket of her ski pants. "Stop it. I'm ticklish."

"Too much information," Crista muttered. "Where's your damn phone?"

Dana pushed Crista's hands away, and unzipped her jacket halfway and reached inside the coat to the inside pocket. "Here."

"I don't need it, you do." Crista pushed the power button and shoved it back at Dana. "Make sure you answer it if it rings."

"I'm doing no such thing. The air horn could go off any time, and I'd miss Juan's final event." Dana started to put the phone away, and Crista grabbed her wrist.

"I swear, I will kick your ass if you don't keep that phone in your hand and answer it when it rings." Crista glared. "Trust me, you do not want to piss me off, girlfriend."

"I'm going to put you on my hate list with Gary and Bruce." Dana backed away, shaking her head. "Fine. I'll leave the phone on."

"Fine." Crista brushed her gloved hands together. "Finally."

While she watched the hillside and contemplated Crista's odd behavior, her phone vibrated. She glanced at the screen, not recognizing the number. She looked up at the slope, ignoring the call.

"Dammit, answer the phone," Crista yelled behind her.

Dana pushed her hood off her head, exasperated with Crista's attitude, and pushed the button to shut her up. "Hello?"

"Hey, babe … " Juan said.

Pleasure flooded her body and she warmed. "What are you doing calling me?"

"I've been telling you we'd talk since before we left for Germany, and I know it's not fair to make you wait any longer." Juan paused. "You deserve more from me, so I thought now would be a good time for us to talk."

"Are you crazy?" She squinted, straining to find him on the slope. "You're supposed to be on the platform."

"I am." He laughed. "What better way to get your attention than to stop the Olympics. It's just me and you here, babe."

"Oh my God," she whispered. "You've gone insane."

"No. I've fallen in love with you. From the moment I found you running through the lodge in a wedding dress, it's only been you for me. I want to wake up beside you every morning and hold you every night as we go to sleep," he said.

She pressed her hand to her chest. "Are you serious?"

He chuckled. "As a heart attack. Do me a favor and wave at Bruce for me."

She turned around and found everyone staring at her. Ana wiped her tears. Crista beamed. Maria giggled, covering her mouth. She caught Bruce's gaze and waved, looking at him curiously. "Okay, I waved."

"Good. Is he coming toward you?"

"Yeah." She caught her lip between her teeth.

Bruce lifted her free hand and placed something in it, and curled her fingers. He winked before backing away.

"Babe, open your hand," Juan said softly.

She turned her wrist and opened up her hand. "Oh my God," she whispered.

A gold double ring loaded with more diamonds than she could count sparkled on her glove. She blinked furiously to expel the moisture blurring her vision.

"I realized I never thought to buy you a wedding ring for our fake marriage, and since I want to make this real, I thought you'd like an engagement and wedding ring." He paused. "Dana?"

"What?" she said.

"Will you stay married to me?"

She turned around and gazed up at the platform. She already knew her answer, and she had a feeling he did too. "I'll tell you once you hit the finish line. Now go win the gold."

"Will you be waiting for me?" he asked.

She smiled, clutching the ring to her chest. "Always," she whispered.

Several minutes later, the air horn blared. Dana counted the seconds, and held her breath as Juan shot from the ramp up into the air.

One flip.

Two flip.

A twist.

She gasped, leaning forward as she watched him going for—oh my God—a second full twist.

He moved too fast for her to watch his skis to see if they were aligned, and he descended. Her knees buckled, and she held on to the fence to stay standing. *Come on, honey. Come on …*

Juan straightened into a standing position from a perfect crouched landing. The spectators screamed. The announcer yelled over the loudspeaker, but she tuned everything out. Someone hugged her from behind, but she only had eyes for Juan.

He skied straight for her, never glancing at anyone else. She bounced, waving to him.

Juan skidded to a stop in front of her. She reached over, grabbed his suit, and pulled him closer.

"Yes. Yes, I'll stay married to you," she said.

He kissed her. She clung to him, afraid she'd wake up and find out she'd dreamt the whole dramatic day.

Juan pulled back and put his lips on her ear. "I love you, Mrs. Santiago."

She closed her eyes, and melted. "I love you, Amante Español."

Chapter Twenty-Five

One freaking fantastic month later.

Dana sat on Juan's lap, happier than she could ever remember being. She gazed around the living room at all the friends and family filling the house. Upon arriving back in Oregon after their honeymoon to Italy, she'd quickly settled into Juan's house when Ana announced she was throwing them a reception.

That was yesterday, and the only people who remained were Ana, Maria, Grayson and his wife Shauna, Dominic and his fiancée Diana, Bruce, Crista, and Gary. She'd insisted they all spend the night, so she could get to know them better. It hadn't been hard to convince the girls. They had a lot of conspiring to do about their men.

"My turn to hold the baby." She hopped off Juan's lap.

Maria handed her Grayson and Shauna's baby. She cradled Trevor's head and sighed. No matter how many times she got to hold Trevor, she never tired of looking at him. He simply fascinated her.

From the light, baby blonde fuzz on the top of his head to the sweet scent of baby powder encompassing everything he touched, the child was the most adorable infant she'd ever seen. He took all the strange people holding him with good-natured patience, while they counted his fingers and looked at his toes.

Dana walked over and sat beside Juan. "Isn't he beautiful?"

"Handsome," Grayson said.

Dominic coughed. "Manly."

"Rugged," Bruce said.

"Tough," Gary added.

She glanced at Juan. "Aren't you going to add a description of Trevor to the male mix, so he can grow up to be a famous athlete like his father and all his honorary uncles?"

Juan wiggled his brows. "Studly."

All the females groaned. Dana brought Trevor closer and whispered loud enough everyone could hear her, "Don't you listen too closely to the men in the room. They're all egotistical, dominating, possessive men—" she glanced up and grinned, "who I hope you'll take after when you're all grown up. Just don't grow up too fast, because I like you tiny and adorable."

Trevor gave a wispy baby sigh and his eyelids closed in contentment. She kissed his forehead, inhaling deeply, not ready to see Grayson and Shauna leave and take Trevor with them.

Juan had been right. She'd instantly liked his friends. When she and Juan had stopped at Cottage Grove on their way home from Germany, the girls had taken her out for a drink. Diana, Crista, and Shauna—who'd brought Trevor into the lounge, ignoring the bartender's dirty look when she pulled the plug on the jukebox and ignored the stares as she breastfed in the bar—took her out on what they called "Girls' Night." She'd filled them in on how she'd met Juan. Thankfully, two shots of vodka helped her feel like she and Juan had started off like any normal couple.

Compared to Shauna and Diana's stories, her marriage to Juan was easy.

"What're your plans now that you've retired from competing, Juan?" Dominic put his arm around Diana. He tugged one of her curls, and grinned down at her.

"I've signed a five year contract to be a spokesman for the National Ski Association and I'll be doing some motivational speaking with minority groups all across the states and visiting the classrooms." Juan gazed down at the baby, who he'd coerced into gripping his pinky.

"Five years?" Gary shifted in the chair. "That's an odd length for a contract."

Juan lifted his gaze to Dana and winked. "We've got a schedule to keep."

Dana brought the baby up to her chest and cuddled him. No matter how many times she'd told Juan her life schedule was unimportant, he stood firm that he liked the idea of knowing what to expect. They wanted children of their own eventually, and five years seemed like a perfect time to settle down for both of them.

The doorbell rang.

Juan stood. She gazed after him, enjoying the way he strutted across the room. Whether he was in a crowd or at home, he was in his element and content. Not to mention smokin' hot.

It was still hard for her to believe he was hers, and she could kiss him whenever she wanted. She'd quickly learned that he loved kissing her about as much as he enjoyed sex.

Juan stepped back into the room. "Dana?"

"Yes?" She handed the baby to Shauna. "Who is it?"

Juan stepped aside, and her father walked into the living room. Dana hurried forward.

Colton Reese stood scanning the room in his navy suit and red power tie. At sixty years old, he only had a bit of gray coloring the hair at his temples. For how much he aggravated her, he was her dad and she'd missed seeing him. If she was honest, she'd even missed the daily back and forth as they fought over the right way to do business while she was on her honeymoon.

"Daddy, you made it." Dana hugged him, and spotted more people coming in the door. She squealed, and grabbed her stepbrothers, forcing them to put up with her kisses. She even hugged Linda, her stepmom, and received a kiss on her cheek in return. "I can't believe you came. This is perfect."

"Of course we came. You're my daughter." Her dad straightened his suit jacket.

Juan made introductions, and Dana caught up with her brothers. She promised them all they could go swimming in the indoor pool to escape the adults, and laughed as they ran out of the room to discover the rest of the house.

"We're sorry we didn't make it to the party yesterday, but we just got back home," Linda said.

"That's okay. Bad planning on our part, but we knew our only chance to get away was right after Juan tied up all his post-Olympic interviews. Besides, you made it now. That's all that's important." She moved over to stand by Juan, slipping her arm around his waist and leaning into him.

"What location are you going to work from now that you live in Oregon? Or are you going back to Colorado?" Dad asked her. "Might be best to find an easy commute and stay in the Northwest. I hear Mt. Hood has a rather attractive lodge. You could take a day trip up and check them out. Maybe we can do a shop come this fall."

She glanced at Juan, who'd linked his finger with hers. "I was going to talk to you about my future plans later, Dad."

"No time like the present. Business always comes first. It's the Reese motto you grew up with, girl," Dad said.

"Right." She inhaled swiftly. "Okay. I guess now would be a good time to tell you the news and get it out of the way, so we can enjoy the rest of your visit."

Dad frowned. "Is there a problem?"

"No, not for me personally." She lifted her chin. "But a lot will change for both of us."

Her dad frowned. "What are you saying?"

"I've made other plans for my career, Dad. My letter of resignation with Reese Company will be sent on Monday."

"What?" Her dad crossed his arms. "But you're my top seller. Reese Company needs you."

Shocked to hear him admit it, Dana stepped forward and kissed her dad's cheek. "Thank you, that means the world to me, Daddy."

"You've proven yourself this last year, kiddo. It's nonsense to quit now," Dad said. "If you need me to pat your back, consider it patted. You've quadrupled our sales as a whole this year."

"I'm not quitting the ski industry exactly, but going in a different direction." She smiled up at Juan. "I'm going into business for myself. I've prototyped my own line of skis—I've been working during my free time for the last several years to perfect what I believe will be the top line equipment in years to come—and will be selling the catalogue come spring. I learned the business from the best man I know and even though we'll be in direct competition, I hope you can be proud of me and wish me well."

"Impossible." Dad shook his head. "You don't have enough money to start your own business from scratch, and I'm not going to set you up only to have you lose the money I'd be investing in you. Unless your husband is financially backing you, there's no way for you to bank a startup company."

"Dana is the prime owner, and although I support her one hundred percent, she's financially supporting herself with no outside interest. I'm only here to help sponsor her line through the sport." Juan put his arm around her shoulders. "I'm proud of what she's accomplished."

"But … how?" Her dad frowned.

"Juan took the money you paid him when we got married and put it in an account with only my name on it. He doesn't want a dime for marrying me." Dana curled against Juan, and laid her hand on his stomach. "He gave it back to me as a wedding gift for marrying him."

Her stomach quivered. She'd always remember that day. Knowing he wanted no part in her father's attempt to see her married pleased her.

Her dad reached over and shook Juan's hand. "Well played, son. I knew from the time she was sixteen she'd give me a run for my money. I'm glad to see she has a good man to back her, and you did the right thing. Welcome to the family."

Juan shook her father's hand. "Thank you, sir."

Dana's jaw dropped, and she quickly recovered, motioning them into the room. "Sit, I'll grab you something to drink."

She slipped into the kitchen alone and leaned against the counter. Overwhelmed with everything happening, she wasn't sure if she'd handled sharing the news the right way. She swallowed hard. Her dad supported her?

She never thought she'd see the day that Daddy backed her decision in anything, much less business. She'd purposely kept her plans to herself for fear of rejection, and he'd known all along. It almost sounded like he'd set her up by giving Juan the money to test him ... and he'd passed.

Juan walked into the kitchen. "Babe? Are you okay?"

She was now. She smiled, walking into his embrace. "I'm wonderful."

"Good." He kissed the tip of her nose. "Do you think once everyone goes home, we can spend some time together, just the two of us?"

"I think I can pencil you in, honey," she whispered.

She grinned, remembering how two months ago, she would've had to check her schedule before answering. Those days were long gone. She enjoyed the spontaneity that came with being married to Amante Español.

More from This Author
(From *Seductively* by Debra Kayn)

If Stan Dogger raised his voice any louder, Diana Spenner was going to scream. It was bad enough he decided to call her out on her last hour of working before her two weeks of vacation started, but she had no desire to tell the hotel owner the real reason she wanted to continue working and skip her down time.

Except she had a little thing called a temper, and Mr. Dogger had used his quota of bossiness for the day. She clamped her lips. *Let it go, let it go …*

"You're going to die of a heart attack if you keep working every day without a break." Mr. Dogger fisted his hands on his waist.

Oh, now he was just being ridiculous. "I'm twenty-four. I'm not going to keel over because I like working a forty-hour week. Besides, I already promised I'd take a couple of weeks off in the spring, before tourist season starts." She smiled extra wide, hoping against the odds he'd change his mind.

"That's six months away," he said.

"Come on, Mr. Dogger." She lowered her voice and stepped closer. "Admit it. You need me here. You don't want to cover for me. Mrs. Dogger wants to take you to Napa Valley for a week. It'd be the perfect time to get away, enjoy the sunshine, drink some wine, and buy your wife those fancy red heels she's eyed at Sallie's Shoes."

His bushy gray brows lowered. "I've known you since you were a little girl. Don't be using my wife against me. If I hear you've conspired behind my back with Adele, I'll fire you. Now, go home!"

She scoffed. "Fine. I expect you to call me if things get too hectic. I'll even fill in for one of the servers in the lounge if anyone calls in sick."

As the hotel manager, she usually oversaw the front desk, scheduled the other employees, and made sure the guests were enjoying their stay without any complaints. But, she wasn't going to turn down extra work if she could convince Mr. Dogger to fit her in elsewhere at the hotel. With tourist season upon them, he could use the extra help.

"Get out of here." He pointed to the doorway. "Go. Not another word."

Discouraged, she gathered her laptop and fled the office. She'd counted on working the extra hours and taking her vacation pay at the same time. The money from earning double time wages would've set her a month ahead of schedule on her dream of purchasing the old Ferriday place. That'd move her next goal of opening a bed and breakfast up to next summer. Now she was going to have to wait until December to purchase the house, and hope that no one bought it in the meantime.

Of course, she couldn't tell Mr. Dogger why she wanted to work. Soon, she'd be his only competition in the small valley. The less people knew of her plans, the better.

She wasn't going to let anyone talk her out of doing what she wanted. One word about her decision to spend her savings, and her parents would do whatever they could to discourage her. That's why she'd deposited her money at the Cottage Grove Credit Union, and not her father's bank across the street. She even refused to mention a word about her dreams to her best friends, Shauna and Kate, and she usually never kept anything secret from them.

A woman's loud scream came from behind her. She whirled around and barely jumped out of the way of three women running toward the lobby. Clutching her laptop to her chest, she gazed after them. Something exciting must have happened in the otherwise quiet town.

She followed them at a slower pace, arriving in the front of the hotel to find a packed room. She studied the area, and frowned.

It seemed every woman staying at the hotel had gathered in front of her.

The last time she saw this big of a crowd was during the Cottage Grove Fundraiser two months ago when Dominic Chekovsky, a professional hockey player, made an appearance in public. The hair at the back of her neck moved as another woman ran past her to enter the large group congregating in front of the double glass doors. She shivered as a bad feeling came over her, one Shauna would say was a cosmic sign from Jupiter that a major roadblock was headed her way.

Silence swept through the crowd, and the cluster of women parted in what she'd call quiet reverence. She squinted, peering around the shoulders of the women. A ball of foreboding settled under her ribs, followed by a gasp. She refused to call her reaction an adrenaline rush or an attraction that threatened to careen out of control.

She'd barely accepted the reality of seeing the biggest pain in her ass when Dominic Chekovsky strolled across the blue carpet in all his six foot four glory, straight toward her. His blond hair short and swept to the side framed a face women could only call stunning. The angled cheeks, dominant chin, all atop broad shoulders, slim waist, and thick thighs. He really was a nicely sculpted man, until he opened his mouth.

His eyes so light blue, they appeared more ice-like, gave him an intense gaze. A gaze he directed straight at her.

She stood straighter and lifted her chin. A week ago, she'd punched him in the stomach when he wouldn't move out of her way and accept she wasn't interested in dating him. This time, if he refused to take no for an answer, she'd hit him over his hard head with her laptop. Then sue him for damages. She had no interest in dating a professional athlete. Especially one with an ego bigger than the stadium or coliseum or whatever kind of building hockey players played in.

She'd witnessed how women reacted to him. She would never lower herself to scream and claw over anyone, no matter how sexy he was in person.

"Diana. It's so good to see you again." Dominic stopped in front of her.

"What are you doing here?" She stepped back when the women pressed in on all sides of her.

"I must talk with you." He ignored the other women. "Maybe somewhere we can be alone without an audience. Please?"

His Russian accent was thick, each word pronounced with emphasis as if he meant to hold his audience captive. She glanced around and rolled her eyes. Each woman crowded around him held their breath, waiting for him to give them each a bit of personal attention.

"It's important, Diana," he said.

"I don't believe you." She waved her hand dismissively. "Take your pick, stud. Any one of them would love to spend time with you and listen to what you have to say."

The crowd vibrated with tension. She fought the urge to tell them all to get a life. It was utterly ridiculous seeing grown women, most of them married, throwing themselves in Dominic's path.

"Shauna told me to tell you it was in your best interest to talk with me." Dominic inched forward.

She groaned. He knew using Shauna, who'd do anything for Diana, as a pawn would work. Damn him.

Mr. Dogger was going to throw a fit when he hears about the disturbance Dominic was causing in the hotel again. He still hadn't forgiven Dominic for the damage the women caused last time he came to town. Although, the extra money Dominic gave Mr. Dogger for the damage the women caused in their attempt to get to him ended up providing new tables in the lounge.

If Diana took him upstairs to her room at the hotel, the women would follow and never leave the vicinity. She caught her bottom lip between her teeth. Mr. Dogger would have no other option than to have her continue working after he realized the women would not leave as long as Dominic was here.

"Fine. You can come with me up to my room. Ten minutes. And you're not allowed to ask me out on a date." She pushed her way through the crowd, letting Dominic find his own way of keeping up with her.

In the elevator, she held her laptop in front of her body as a shield and kept the women from following them inside. Dominic squeezed past her. The doors slid closed, and she pushed the button, sending them up to the next floor, and relaxed.

"Thanks." Dominic leaned against the wall.

She watched the floor lights climb above the door. "Just so you know, I didn't do this for you. It's for Shauna."

"You wound me."

"You'll survive." She watched the lights climb above the doors. "This is my floor."

He followed her out of the elevator and down the hall. She shifted the laptop under her arm, and felt Dominic take it from her grasp. Without arguing over being perfectly fine managing on her own, she dug the key out of her pocket.

Most hotels upgraded to card keys years ago, but Mr. Dogger kept the old hotel to the original construction since he bought the place back in the seventies. She was lucky enough to convince him to change over to using computers six months ago to make her job easier.

The elevator pinged the second she swung the door open and the giggles from the women following them pushed her into action. She shoved Dominic inside before locking the door. The rumors of women, all women, being highly attracted to the star were no exaggeration. She'd seen the mobs that followed him, touched him without permission, and how the females threw themselves on him at the fundraiser. Later when she'd hung out with her friends at the Quayside, Dominic had to leave early because the women were causing a scene.

A small part of her could almost feel sorry for him. She took her laptop from him, set it on the table, and crossed her arms. "Okay, you've got ten minutes to say what you think is so important you had to interrupt my perfectly fine day."

She rarely invited anyone into her private room. Despite living in a hotel, she'd made the place her own. Plants lined the floor near the patio sliding door leading to the balcony. She'd bought fabric and covered the couch and chair with a floral print to brighten the room, and placed a few large wicker baskets around the sparse area that held her personal belongings. She might live in a hotel, but she needed her books, her CD's, and her sketchbook of the plans she was drawing.

She tilted her head and studied him. "Well? Are you going to tell me why you came to see me?"

Dominic's brow wrinkled and he stared at her before catching himself and walking across the room to peer out of the window. She waited. Her experience with Dominic usually caused her to become defensive, and him to lay everything out on the line.

Ever since he'd come to Cottage Grove—at her friend Shauna and her boyfriend, Grayson Schyler's request—he'd set out to sweep Diana off her feet. He was dominating and bossy, and no matter how many times she explained she wasn't interested in going out on a date, he became more determined to get her to change her mind. She had no idea how to get through to him.

She was not interested in dating him. Brent Thiegher, her college boyfriend, acted the same way. She'd dated him for over a year, despite knowing he was a flirt. All she saw was a star quarterback, sexy, popular, and smooth talker. One month after she broke up with him, knowing she'd never be happy in a relationship with him, she found out he'd seen three other women while they were supposed to be exclusive.

She eyed Dominic. He was a pro hockey player, sexy, popular, and a smooth talker too. Normally he had no problems bossing his way into a conversation. Today, his quietness unsettled her. Where was the charm? The flirting? The massive dose of self-confidence?

She moved over and sat on the edge of the couch. The subdued attitude bothered her. Something must've happened to —

She jumped to her feet. "Oh my God, is Shauna okay?"

He turned around. "Of course. I'm staying at Grayson's house. I saw her this morning before she went to work."

She sat back down. "And Grayson is okay too?"

"He's fine." Dominic walked across the room and sat on the other end of the couch, well away from her.

"Why are you back?" She gripped the cushion underneath her, knowing she sounded bitchy but unable to stop. Dominic needed no encouragement from her, or he'd assume she'd changed her mind about him. He'd be wrong.

She had no desire to go out with him. None. Ever. Not even if he begged. Okay, she might like to see him on his knees. Maybe then the women would stop throwing themselves at him if they saw a little humbleness thrown in with his huge ego.

She inhaled, catching a hint of spicy cologne. Her stomach fluttered, and she shook her head to snap out of finding him attractive. "Are you going to answer my question?"

He leaned forward and planted his elbows on his knees. "I need your help."

He joked. Her burst of laughter dwindled, until she frowned. This man had everything going for him. Fame, skills, wealth, and not to mention any woman he wanted at his fingertips. Why would he need her help?

All he had to do was ask people, and anyone would help him. He was famous. He even had a security team he usually took with him when out in public who helped him keep his distance from all the women who ran after him. She'd seen him handle himself just fine when he was around his friends.

"Come on, Dominic, talk. You're taking up my vacation time." She crossed her legs.

"Has anyone told you that you're pushy?

"All the time." She shrugged. "Why?"

"It's very attractive."

She snorted. "The answer's no."

"You don't know what I was going to ask you," he said.

"Let's see … " She swung her foot back and forth. "You're going to ask me out. That's what you do every time you see me, and my answer is still no."

He sighed and sat back, staring straight ahead and not looking at her. She studied his profile. His jaw twitched and he ran his hands along the length of his thighs. She gulped. Long, hard, thick thighs a woman could dig her nails into.

"Hockey season has started and I'd like you to come and stay with me at my place," he spoke quietly.

She shook her head in surprise. "So you're skipping dating and going straight to sex. The answer's still no. You do nothing for me."

God, she was a liar. He could do a lot for her, but thinking about *it* was different than actually doing *it*.

"Please." He shifted and faced her. "The women are affecting my playing. I have a company who keeps trying to steal my towels. I can't even sleep at night, because the coach said I have to make them all go away. I don't know how. You're the only one who can't stand me."

"Why do you think I can help you or I'd want to help? I don't even like you because you think everyone wants you."

"They do." His brows lowered and he sighed.

She shook her head. "That's why you irritate me."

"I have a proposition for you. I want you to pretend to be my girlfriend. Maybe you'll scare the women away. They're the source of my problem. They won't leave me alone. Day and night, they're finding new ways to get close to me. I need them to go away." The sincerity written on his face showed her he wasn't joking around.

"Get real."

He shook his head. "You don't get it. If I can figure out why you don't like me, I can use that knowledge to get the cologne company off my back. That will also make the women disappear from my life and leave me in peace, so I can concentrate on playing hockey."

"Cologne?"

"They think my sweat turns women on and want to bottle my ... smell."

She stared. "That's disgusting."

"You're telling me. Try having your boxers stolen when you slip into the showers after practice or someone trying to lift your luggage at the airport." He stood and paced the room. "I can't stand it anymore." Her phone rang. She walked over and looked at the screen. *Yes!*

Mr. Dogger already needed her. *Goodbye, vacation. Hello, Ferriday house.* "Hang on a second. I need to take this."

She pushed the button. "Hello, Mr. Dogger. How are you?"

He rattled in her ear in short sentences, his voice rising. She grinned and shimmied around the table. "I'll be happy to help you. That'll be double time. I'm on vacation, remember?"

She disconnected the call and squealed. Halfway to the door, she remembered Dominic and paused. "I'm sorry. I need to go back to work. Good luck with your problem."

Dominic hurried over and blocked the door. "I'll pay you five hundred thousand dollars to spend the next two weeks with me at my home, so I can continue to play hockey."

Her head snapped back and she blinked. A half a million dollars?

"You're joking."

"There's nothing funny about my life." He dropped his arms to his sides. "You're my only hope, or I'm going to give up hockey completely and go back to Russia. At least there, I can live in peace. I'm desperate, Diana."

There was no denying he had money, and she knew how much playing hockey meant to him. She bit down on her bottom lip. With that much money, she could quit her job, buy the Ferriday house, and be open for business in no time. Best of all, she'd be debt free and wouldn't have to take out a loan, which would make her parents proud of her.

But she'd have to put up with Dominic for two weeks. She'd end up killing him within three days. She ground her teeth together. It would test all her patience, but she would have more than enough money if she survived staying with him with her sanity intact.

She didn't have to think twice. The Ferriday house was her dream. "I'll do it."

Also available from this author: Breathing His Air and *Wildly*
In the mood for more Crimson Romance?
Check out *Change My Mind*
by Elley Arden
at *CrimsonRomance.com.*